The Seed

Written by
Charlie Bawksochawkolitz

Copyright- Alcyone Press ink.

Contact: CB @theseedofeden.net

The Seed is a semi-science-fictional comic-tragic-romance mystery-drama and expositional musical autotomic-biography.

Our hero is a middle-aged chess master who travels to Barcelona Spain to compete in the 2022 World Chess tournament championship. He has been given a message in a flash drive from his Uncle who died in 1963 and finds that he has been recruited to engage in a mission calling him to commit a great sacrifice for all of humanity.

After a series of enlightening encounters our hero falls in love with the brilliant and gifted chess master Ingrid Orsic of Munich Germany. Her great grandmother Maria Orsic founded the Vril Society, a secret order of matriarchs that let their hair grow long for psychic purposes, re-embracing the sacred feminine.

She has been assigned to guide Robert towards his higher calling through transcendental means. Their destinies become intertwined in the most complex and spiritually sanctimonious manner, yet reluctantly accepting of their mission impossible.

Our hero finds that he is carrying the blood of sacred line of ancestry and will need to set it into stone before he leaves this world but finds himself running out of time. He is set to face off with Sophie, the Artificial Intelligent Robot, in an existential level 1-hour runoff chess match on the world stage

Keep in mind as you go forward into this adventure that I have laced the story line with much humor. You should find it to be a fine blend and healthy balance of tragedy and comedy

"We are stardust, we are golden, we are a billion-year-old carbon and we've got to get ourselves back to the garden."

                Joni Mitchell

"You're packing a suitcase for a place that none of us has been. A place that has to be believed… to be seen. You could have flown away… a singing bird in a cage… who will only fly… only fly, for freedom…. walk on…walk on, stay safe tonight."

                Paul David Hewson

"Let fury have the hour, anger can be power. You know that you can use it."

                Joe Strummer

*You I stung
with poisoned tongue.
In jest,
of course.
Must I be cursed
for a line unrehearsed.
If time were reversed
I would take it back.*

*Forgiveness is the Key to Salvation.
Gratitude to All.
We are cells in the greater body of God.*

TABLE OF CONTENTS

1	PANIC IN BOSTON	1
2	AUTOPILOT	6
3	MEMORY	10
4	FLASH	16
5	GAUDI	21
6	SOPHIE	32
7	VRIL	39
8	MAGNUS	46
9	DOUBLE-ELIX	54
10	THE SECRET	61
11	QUARTERS	63
12	EYE SPY	71
13	MANDELLA	77
14	DREAM POLICE	83
15	TAXI	86
16	POSSIBILITIES	89
17	STARRY KNIGHT	93
18	CHARLIE	98
19	SIXTY-THREE	102
20	FORTY-SEVEN	107
21	THIRTY	112
22	X MINUS Y = Q	120
23	KEYHOLE	123
24	ZYGOTE	134
25	KING OF KINGS	138
26	A REAL RAIN	142
27	HOURGLASS	146
28	FINAL STRAW	144
29	END GAME	149
30	THERE HAS TO BE CLOUDS	162

Chapter 1
Panic in Boston

"Sir, as you may have heard, there was recently a security breach affecting most major networks. We have secured our control systems and hope to be back online shortly. Which arrangement works best for you, sir. Munich on the ninth or Frankfurt on the tenth? We will credit your account for this flight due to our systems breakdown."

"I appreciate that and thank you. Munich will be fine. What time is the flight?"

"Departure time is 3:12pm. Here is your boarding pass, sir. Enjoy your flight and please fly us again at AirLingus.com."

Bob grabs a cappuccino for his wait at the gate.

Bob was one of those guys that wore his emotions on his forehead. He had a tough time hiding the fact that he was deathly afraid of flying. A fear not so much akin to the same horrors that many other flyers feel when they envision themselves in a freefall descent into the ocean or downward spiraling interface with the side of a mountain. It was more like that feeling you get when you are being set into a precisely calculated to receive its maximum number of contents as humanly possible, as in a neatly packed can of sardines.

1

When Bob was seven, he got himself stuck in the dryer looking for his sneakers after school one day. He had climbed in, closing the door and could not get out. You know, one of those kiddie sticky fly traps from the 50's and 60's.

They finally tossed them all in the landfills, good riddance. His older brother did save his life, fortunately, setting him free after two hours of living hell.

Anyways, he does not like confined spaces, kind of a claustrophobe you might call him.

He never seems to forget to pack his Bose sound reduction hi-fi stereo wireless headphones for a flight. This time however, he packed them in his check-in instead of his carry-on. He was just now realizing what he had done.

This spiritually debilitating emotionally crippling real time horror show was not going to ruin his flight, so he told himself. He briskly scans the terminal looking to see if anyone who was wearing headphones may be wanting to sell in a consensual agora style free trade transaction for an even exchange of value, whereas Bob would become the recipient of said headphones.

All he needed was to approach one of these fine travelers and with just one look they would surely see that he was clearly a victim of claustrophobic paranoia and only required just this one simple transaction which would facilitate the proper amount of sedation and pacification enabling him to remain cool, calm, collected and not kill any other passengers during this 8-hour direct no-layovers flight to Barcelona.

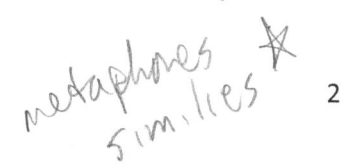

Bob began to sink into his own shadow, cringing as he played out this horrific scene in his head. It had already happened once before on his trip to Mexico City.

He remembers the incident clearly, remanifesting it into his mind's eye, like a Cameo theater-projector man setting the reels in motion. He remembers the ten trips to the bathroom, the twelve walks around the cabin, seven times being told get back to your seat.

The empathic identification he felt not unlike that of a Siberian tiger endlessly pacing, searching for an escape route, a chink in the armor, relief from an unforgiving and merciless enslavement that only his Bose sound reduction hi-fi stereo wireless headphones could remedy.

He spots an older woman sitting two rows over wearing what appeared to be a nice set. Checking his phone for his running out of options margin, he sees that he needs to act quickly.

Brushing off his last-ditch effort brainstorm of sneaking out onto the tarmac, crawling up into the baggage compartment, locating his check-in bag, rescuing his Bose sound reduction hi-fi stereo wireless headphones, and returning to the terminal without getting busted by security, all in time to make his flight.

"Excuse me, Ma'am, I know this is a huge request, but I was hoping to buy your headphones at whatever price you ask, say $300 or so, in cash or bitcoin, if you are willing to part with them. You have no idea how important this is for me," Bob pleading.

"You see... I left my headphones in my check-in bag by mistake. I suffer from claustrophobic episodes and long flights make me very uneasy, making the other passengers around me very uneasy as well. All I need is a good pair of headphones that will be ok for this eight-hour nonstop flight to Barcelona."

"No, thanks," said the woman as she sat unmoving and coldly oblivious to Bob's dire situation, callously ignoring the fact that his ability to remain on this side of socially accepted civil behavior had become severely compromised.

"Ma'am, five hundred."

"No, I'm sorry."

"600 dollars."

"No sir, sorry."

"Flight 369 to Barcelona is now boarding," alerts the flight announcer PA lady.

"One thousand, last offer. Please Ma'am."

"You've got a deal young man. I'll take hundreds."

Bob peels off ten C-notes and hands them over this hideous imposter. What originally appeared to be a nice little old lady, proved to be nothing more than a greedy opportunist. He grabs the headphones away from her. *She ain't no lady.* He turns away and heads towards his gate.

His adrenaline output was a little over the daily recommended dosage, visibly unsettled as he approaches the gate check-in clerk, and hands her his boarding pass and license.

"Good afternoon. Is everything ok, Mr. Dyer?"

"Yes, I'm fine. I just had a little, I mean, nothing, I'm sorry… fine thank you."

"Are you sure, Mr. Dyer? "

Bob nods up and down.

"Mr. Dyer… enjoy your flight."

"My cousin Ricky Reese is the pilot today," he offers up to the clerk, like a little kid trying to change the subject after getting caught misbehaving.

"Glad to hear that. Captain Reese is a wonderful pilot, one of our finest. Enjoy your flight, sir."

As he makes his way through the terminal connector tube hanging his head.

"Mr. Dyer, Mr. Dyer," he turns to see the ticket lady passing him his…. "You dropped your headphones. Enjoy your flight, sir."

Feeling like a complete buffoon now, he makes his way to his seat. "Great, a window."

Slumping down, closing his eyes, and massaging his temples, he slips off into wonderland.

Chapter 2
Sky Pilot

Bob wakes to find his headphones gone. He looks all around the floor and under his seat, "They're nowhere to be found. They're gone." He jumps up and yells; "Who the hell took my headphones, which one of you took them?"

Looking around the cabin he sees several passengers staring at him.

"Hey... sit down," someone yells. "No one took your headphones Pal, sit down. I saw you drop them when you were getting on the plane."

"Those weren't mine. Which one of you took them?"

Passengers started taking off their headphones and hurling them towards Bob. One cracks him off the side of the head. He turns and, in a Bruce Lee-style lightning quick maneuver, grabs the phones as they bounce off his skull. "These are not mine," pointing to the guy that told him to sit down, "Who took them, was it you?"

The flight attendants were now rushing down the aisles as the passengers began to surround him. He lashes out and starts swinging the headphones at the angry mob that were now trying to get at him.

"Which one of you has my god-damned headphones? I need them, I need them now. Whoever took them is responsible for all of this, not me."

"Sir, please sit down. You will be removed from the plane if you do not sit back down."

Becoming even more enraged, he starts screaming at the flight attendants who were trying to push their way through. "Someone took my headphones. One of your passengers took them, and they are going to pay, Ricky will make them pay."

As the attendants got to within his reach, he pulls himself up grabbing onto the overhead compartment ledge, then lifting his torso, he starts kicking and thrashing at his assailants.

Then in mosh-pit style, he begins crawling and stepping over their heads, jumping across the middle row, landing into the left side aisle, he sprints towards the front of the plane, "Ricky, stop the plane! Someone took my headphones!"

As he approaches the attendant station, he sees his cousin Ricky stepping out from the cockpit door.

"I have your headphones, Bob," Ricky said, smiling as he turns around and pulls them onto his head, then starts snapping his fingers, swiveling his hips, and swoons his way back into the cockpit. Bob's jaw drops: "Cousin Ricky, you son of a bitch."

He pulls the fire extinguisher from the wall as it was the closest most accessible make-shift weapon immediately at his disposal, then charges into the cockpit, seeing that the windshield had blown out and Ricky was out on the nose of the plane dancing to MC Hammer.

"You can't touch this," Ricky sang out, laughing, dancing, and waving his arms, pointing to Bob.

"Ricky why are you doing this to me, I always liked and trusted you, why?"

"Bob you need to take over the plane now, it is up to you to save all these people. I get off here," Ricky instructs and then steps off the nose of the plane and free-falls out of sight.

    Bob looks around the cockpit in panicked desperation, sitting in the captain's chair were his headphones. He sits down, puts them on, and stares out into the open sky ahead.

"Bob, push down on the wheel, lower your speed with the stick shift device, gently pull it towards you, then push the red flashing button above the visor," said the voice coming through his headphones.

"Ricky is that you?"

"Bob, save these people, push the red button."

    Bob pulls down the visor and pushes the red flashing button. Immediately a loud whooshing sound fills the cockpit. He turns to see an inflatable doll expand into the co-pilots chair. The fully-inflated plasticine turns to Bob and says: "I've got this Bob. You can take your seat now."

As Bob turns to leave the cockpit, the vinyl pilot snatches the fire extinguisher out of his hand, knocking him out, settling him down into the captain's chair.

Chapter 3
Memory

"Sir... wake up."

Bob feels a slight nuzzle on his shoulder, opening one eye, "Sir, we have landed, you must exit the plane now. Welcome to Barcelona."

Bob composes himself, then secures his belongings and exits the plane.

"There you are, I thought you hated flying. You're usually the first to get off the plane," Ricky chortles. "Why don't we walk out together and share a taxi to our hotel."

"Whoa... Ricky, I'm sorry, I just woke up. Sure... let me grab an espresso on our way out. I'll be... uh...that would be fine."

Bob was still lingering in the nightmare he experienced during his eight-mile-high nap. He had never slept through an entire flight before.

"You're going to love Barcelona," Ricky shares as they hop into their transport. "I have something incredibly special to share with you." Then he directs the driver... "Hotel Catalonia."

"Oh good, here it is." Ricky pulls out an 8.5 by 11 manilla envelope from his briefcase and presents it to Bob.

"What is it?" Bob prodding.

"Open it."

Bob unclips the envelope stay and removes an 8 by 10 black and white photo.

"That's your Uncle Paul, Aunt Mary and this guy over here," Ricky points to the distinguished well-kept gentleman standing next to Mary, "is General Max Taylor. He was one of dad's closest companions. They both served in World War two together in strategic planning and intelligence and were Masters of Data collection and code breaking. Max was a lieutenant back then working for IBM as their Military Intelligence liaison.

"They worked side by side for several years applying state of the art data collection and analysis techniques, utilizing improving and re-engineering hardware technologies, and instituting new and more sophisticated operating systems language."

Bob pointing down, "When was this picture taken?"

"That is our summer cottage in Yarmouth. I believe this was '49 or '50, not sure, but do you notice anything?"

"Yes, it's like I am peering into a looking glass. Paul is my spitting image, or I am his."

"Yeah, that's what Pat says. She wants you to give her a call sometime."

"I know, I do need to catch up. I've been so wrapped up getting ready for this tournament that I lost track of time. Promise I'll do better after these matches, promise!"

"She knows, don't worry. They are all rooting for you this weekend. The kids will be looking for a big trophy with your name on it," Ricky cajoles, "Bob Dyer, chess champion of the world. What a nice ring!"

"Her kids are so cute. How old are they now?"

"Cat is 22 and Billy is 17, not so cute anymore but Cat is a beautiful young lady and what a voice on her, like an angel."

"I really do need to catch up, California is so far away though," Bob lamely excuses himself.

"Yeah, and Barcelona's just a short skip and a hop from Braintree," Ricky counters then reaches in and pulls out an. envelope marked 'Bobby', "There is something else in the sleeve."

"What's this?"

"I have no idea. It says Bobby, that must be you."

"No one has called me Bobby since I was seven when I started demanding that I be called Robert or at minimal, Bob, no more Bobby."

Ricky cracks up laughing. "I remember, it was thanksgiving dinner at the Countryside restaurant in Hingham.

'You stuck a walnut up your nose trying to make your little brother laugh so he would spit his cider out. It worked well until we saw you trying to remove it. You started balling and Janet rushed you to the hospital where the nurse simply tweezered them out.

'You were so upset when we got back to the house in Weymouth for not getting any dessert after dinner…' Bobby, calm down, we'll get you a nice bowl of cake and ice cream, ok?' Mary offered you."

"Aunt Mary, please do not call me Bobby anymore. My name is Robert, you can call me Bob, I like Robert best though."

"Pipes burst like a frozen water main, tears and snorts and eggnog were flying all over. You always did find a way to make everyone laugh," Ricky fondly recalls.

"I wasn't joking, I was serious, it worked though. Three months later no one was calling me Bobby anymore, I was Robert now."

Bob glances back at the envelope then the photo, "I wish I were able to get to know your dad a little better. I was only five when he died, amazing the likeness. Was he anything like me?"

"Well… yeah, I guess. He had a great sense of humor like you, he was brilliant and loved computers, and was an expert chess player reaching a 2600 rating at one time, managing to win a couple national titles in his day. Dr. Paul, as they called him, always wished he had more time to pursue tournament chess play, his work was too important though, and sometimes he would be away from home for a year or more," Ricky laments.

"I would love to hear more about his work."

"Well then, I do have a treat for you. Tomorrow we are sitting for lunch with one of Mom and Dad's dearest friends. It's a surprise so don't even ask, you'll see," Ricky concealing.

"Here we are, Hotel Catalonia."

"Enjoy your stay in Barcelona," celebrates the driver in clear English straddling a strong Catalonian undercurrent.

"Why don't you get cleaned up and meet me for dinner. It's only noon, you should get some rest and study your chess moves or just chill out and take a stroll around this beautiful city. I'll meet you in the restaurant across the street at eight," Ricky signals. "I just need to run up to one of the flight attendants' rooms to drop off a scarf that she left on the plane. See you at 8:00 then."

Ricky presses the sixth, then pats Bob on the shoulder, "I get off here," then briskly exits the lift.

Bob sends the elevator to the ninth. Looking down he notices that the ninth-floor button was flickering and smudged in red lipstick marker, *"Ah… déjà vu or what? … Some crazy voodoo Shit be goin' on here."*

Shaking it off quickly, settling into his ninth-floor suite, lying back into his massive hotel mattress with seven recedingly sized pillows all perfectly arranged he smiles as he rolls out the reels in his head.

Captain Ricky, performing such a profound act of heroism and chivalry, the rescuing of an essential fashion accoutrement and its fateful reunion with the wanting, needing, pawning damsel in distress. "Ricky always did have a way with the ladies."

Too restless to sleep, he hops in the shower and into a fresh set of skids, then steps out for a saunter down towards the Marinas.

Chapter 4
Flash

"Bob, over here... Hi Bob, this is my friend Kristi. She is joining us for dinner tonight."

"Hi Kristi, nice meeting you. It must have been nice to get your scarf back so quickly," Bob inserts foot in mouth.

"Ah... no Bob. No, this is Kristi. She lives here in Barcelona," Ricky successfully recovers the fumble. "Kristi is an artist and a playwright. I was just telling her that you are here for the international chess tournament and will be playing against Magnus Carlsen for the title."

"Well... yeah, I sure hope to. I still need to win my way through the qualifying rounds, competition this year is tough. I may not even make it past the first round."

"He's so modest, of course you will Bob," Ricky assuredly reconfirms.

Bob directs to Kristi, "Do you play?"

"*Oui oui.* Yes, but I never win. It is so complex; one bad move and I lose. My brother loves chess, and he is incredibly good, he was high school chess club champion, three years in a row," Kristi peacocks. "I like to paint, write, and produce theater productions."

Bob pursues, "You're a producer?"

"Yes, I am producing a modern version of Cabaret in Paris next month. You should come… I will get you a free pass," Kristi offers.

Bob returns, "I wish I could, but I'll be back home long before then. Well… break a leg as they say or have a great show, bon chance and all that."

Feeling like an interloper, Bob offers up his best remedy, "You know Ricky, Kristi, I must excuse myself," sliding in his chair.

"I'm not really that hungry. I had a late lunch down on the pier and I think the octopus hasn't settled very well. I need to head back to my room and get an early sleep so I can be fresh for our lunch date tomorrow. You two have a great dinner and I'll meet you in the lobby at say noon, Ricky."

"Right! Noon is perfect."

Bob nods, bowing his head, reminiscent of a Buddhist monk humbly addressing his parting.

"*Merci, Bob. Bon chance* and good luck to you, and your chess matches, too."

Bob nodding, "*Merci beaucoup.*"

……..

Bob settles back into his room, opens his laptop, and begins reviewing the Schliemann gambit by injecting optional positional potentials into 'Nikki', his chess game analysis program, that he had been planning to explore.

After a couple of hours of study, strengthening his resolve and confidence, he closes his laptop and gets ready for bed. While pulling off his trousers and emptying his pockets he sees the envelope that he had completely forgotten about.

He slips into his night sweats and decides to see what is inside. Opening the envelope, he discovers that it contains a flash drive. He plugs it in and sees three folders. The first was labeled **47,** the second was 63, and the third was 01.

Separate from the folders was an mpeg file named Bobby. "I'll start with this one," *click click.*

"Hi Bobby, I know you don't barely remember me, I am your uncle Paul Reese, Ricky, and Pat's dad. I have something extremely serious to share with you. This information is not meant to scare, embarrass or harm you in any way, it is meant to enlighten you to your true purpose, your true meaning, and your invaluable importance at this place in time."

Bob watches as his deceased uncle projects this time capsule upon him that must have been sitting on some hard drive somewhere for fifty years or so but somehow made its way onto his laptop.

Being the one and only target for this information transfer, he was beginning to feel special.

"I want you to know how much you meant to me. I wished we could have spent more time together, but as you know life's circumstances press down upon us."

Bob wonders, *where is this all leading?*

"Your mother and I were awfully close. I know you were told that your father died in Vietnam. Well… he did, but he was not your real father. He was an exceptionally good man and he filled in for me as I tried to accommodate the best life for you.

"This may be hard for you to hear but I loved Mary and your mother Janet. I know it wasn't so big of me, pun intended, but you are my son, Ricky is your half-brother, and Pat your half-sister.

"I helped support Janet after your dad died and made sure that you, your mother, and your brothers would never be for want.

"As you know, I died back in November of 1963. I can't explain to you in this message how it is possible that I could make such a claim, predicting the knowledge of my own death. All shall be revealed my son, all shall be revealed.

"You will not be expected to share these revelations with any others, including and especially, Pat and Ricky. They need not to know this. They are happy in their lives and this information for better or worse would disrupt their current paths. It would not benefit them in any way but serve as a detriment to their solid and stable belief systems that allow them to proceed as they are destined to in their present form.

"I recommend that you open folder 63 first, but not until you get to Frankfurt after your tournament.

"I know, I know, What the Fuck! Good luck this Sunday and no, I am not telling you who wins. Have a great time with Ricky tomorrow, he has got a wonderful treat in store for you and for Christ's sakes…call your sister."

Bob rips out the flash drive tossing it into the desk drawer slamming it shut as if thrusting a maggot laced heap of filth down the trash chute, condemning this garbage to an infernal grave.

"What the Fuck is right! Who the hell does he think he is? He can't do this to me. A message from the grave…Jesus! I am going to tell Ricky the whole thing. I want his kids to know what a piece of Shit he really was."

Bob began to sob; he never even met his supposedly real fake dad. His mother must have lived a lie her whole life. Aunt Mary can't have known any of this, or did she?"

"I need more answers. I need to know the truth, the whole truth, and nothing but the truth. I can't let this influence my concentration this weekend. Thanks a lot uncle baby daddy."

Chapter 5
Gaudi

"Gurgle, gurgle…. phwhoosh."

Bob's gullet was an erupting swill, a volcano ready to blow.

He rushes into the bathroom barely quick enough to drop his drawers and release the Kraken. He spends a good 29-minutes purging, rubbing, and wishing he were dead. "Oh my god… I am never eating anything that crawls, slithers, or creeps around this god forsaken planet ever again. Never eat anything that ambulates with more or less than four legs," he advises himself.

He attempts to clean up using the boudais then hops in the shower for nice long hot one. While drying off he looks down into the porcelain bowl examining the aftermath.

"Worst case of splatter jack I've ever seen. I'll need to leave the maid a big tip tonight for sure. Might need a sandblasting crew up here to clean this mess up."

Looking at the time, "It's 3 am. Damn! I need to get some more sleep." He crawls back under the covers and slips back into slumber.

……..

"Ring a ling ... Ring a ling a ring..."

Bob reaches over and sets the receiver down next to his head.

"Mr. Dyer, your cousin Ricky is waiting for you in the lobby. Are you coming down, sir?" inquires the desk clerk.

"Oh Shit, yes. What time is it?"

"Twelve thirty Mr. Dyer, should I tell him you are on your way down to the lobby?"

"No, I mean yes, I just need like say… tell him ten minutes, tell him I'll be right down."

He scrambles his gear into his pack and tosses a hundred on the bathroom counter then scurries out the door.

"Ricky, I'm so sorry, I had a rough night. Could use a nice hot coffee with a cyanide chaser."

"Wow, you do look pale. Maybe you should tuck in your shirt and fix your pant legs."

Bob looks down to see his shirt is untucked, shoes untied, and socks were up over his pant leg cuffs. "Oh boy… where is that Kevorkian cappuccino? Might be the right time."

Ricky chuckles, "You'll be fine, stop beating yourself up. You should have seen me when I did a layover in Nagasaki, I went for dinner with these two twin sisters I met at the hotel and had the blowfish for dinner. Now I know why they call it that. My two-night layover turned into a ten-day hospital visit. I believe I died eight times that week or at least prayed for it. Death, where is thy sting, I repeated over and over and over."

Bob anguishing, "So where are we going today? I'm not so sure I can eat anything today, tomorrow, in a week, a month, this year, never mind lunch in two hours."

"First I want to show you an amazing museum uptown," Ricky remedies.

……..

"Here we are, the Gaudi House museum, wait 'til you see the interactive self-touring audio and visual guide, it's trippy," Ricky delights.

"Hold up your smart phone and point towards the walls and windows as you walk through the rooms to see the interactive visual display," the Gaudi House tour guide instructs.

"Wow, can you see this, there are sea turtles swimming around the room… crazy cool. This architecture is amazing. I see how Gaudi incorporated the natural world into his creations."

"Yeah, I know, amazing isn't it. Let's head upstairs." Ricky leads the climb as they explore every nook and cranny ascending to the rooftop patio.

"The tiles on this roof look like the scales of a dragon's back," Bob excites. "And just look at this view, such a gorgeous city."

Tourists were meandering about the terrace, Bob was commissioned to perform some camera work for a small group of Asians, "Smile. Cheese," *Click, Click.*

"Thank you."

"De nada."

After a few minutes, Ricky notices that the roof-deck was now clear and vacant. He walks over to a door in the corner and with his index finger's knuckle, taps 3 quick taps, then 6, then 9, the door opens.

A little old lady greets them, "Come in, come in, we have been waiting for you, you are late."

Ricky enters willfully, while Bob hesitates at the door, peering inside before committing.

"We're sorry, Bob had a rough night. It appears that he got himself into a tangle with an octopus yesterday and needed extra time for healing," Ricky covers.

"Quick, close the door, the museum is still open. Please come in and sit."

Bob feeling the urgency for privacy obligingly closes the door and asks, "Where should I sit?"

"Set the bolt and come sit over here at the table, both of you. Bob would you like a cup of tea, it is sure to settle your stomach?"

"If you think it will help, I'll try anything."

"Bob, this is Lydia Taylor, Max's wife."

"Nice to make your acquaintance Lydia," Bob offers his respects. "You live here, in a museum?"

"Yes, we do."

"We?"

"Here Bob, sip your tea, then we can have lunch. Ricky would you like a cup too?"

"Please… could I have some honey and a squeeze of lemon too."

Bob sipping, "This is really good. What kind of tea is it?"

"I call it Elix tea, short for elixir. It is my own recipe of herbs, leaves, roots, barks, and several other secret ingredients. It will rejuvenate, illuminate and is a remedy for a constipate," Lydia giggles.

"You said we, does someone else live here?"

"Ricky, could you take a sip of your tea please."

Ricky raises his cup but stops halfway then freezes, as if he suddenly had become catatonic.

"Hi Bob, so glad to see you."

Bob hears a strong male voice coming from somewhere but could not find its source.

"Bob, raise up your phone and point it at the rocking chair in the corner."

Bob obligingly aims his smartie towards the rocker… "Now you can see me."

Sure enough, there he was, sitting in the chair, but only through the view of his device screen could he see the man. "I am Max, your father's best friend. Ricky brought you here to meet with us. We have so much to share with you today."

Bob glances over to see that Ricky had not budged one inch from his frozen position. "What's wrong with Ricky? What did you do to him?"

"Oh... he'll be fine, he's merely suspended in the flux zone of the time wave cycles.

"At the top and bottom of every time wave cycle is a flux zone, a nano moment, where time is neither moving forward nor backwards. We can talk now, and he will not hear a thing. The information I am sharing with you is not for him. You drank some tea, correct?"

"Yes, it's very tasty, and Lydia is right, I feel rejuvenated, and my gut feels great now."

"Lydia is always right. Her tea is a combination of the most healing elements on earth. She has mastered the formula, which includes as she stated, all-natural ingredients, including colloidal silver, gold, platinum, iridium, and a tinge of Datura Stramonium.

"This concoction is a long-forgotten brew originally used by the pharaohs of ancient Egypt. It provides strength, wisdom, longevity and best of all, it connects the voids in our DNA structures, reconnecting the strands of the double helix, enabling a much fuller access to our true potential by illuminating and electrifying these connections, resulting in greater awareness, intelligence, and fortitude.

"The so-called junk DNA is not junk at all. Ours has been tweaked and manipulated by other races of beings to remove our higher potentials by shutting off access to almost 90% of our genes. These off-world beings needed a slave race to perform their dirty work here on earth.

"Our source creator will not allow this to be mankind's destiny. We were given free will, we know right from wrong, we choose our futures, but with these imposed limitations, we cannot achieve our greatest God-given potentials.

"This Elix tea is the best tool we have for raising our vibrations and opening new and wonderful possibilities for us all. Lydia and I were hoping that you will help us get this tea into the right hands, bellies, and minds.Now here comes the big one, have another sip or two before we get going."

Bob takes two more quick sips then downs the entire drink.

Max continues, "Humanity is at a crossroads in our development, we are facing head on an existential threat that is completely avoidable, unlike a pole shift, a meteorite collision, or a solar flash, which are unpredictable events, few and far between and completely out of our control, we can stop this one by simply pulling the plug."

Bob began to resonate at an unprecedented rate, like a clairvoyant he was beginning to anticipate Max's words before they even came out, "You're talking about Artificial Intelligence, aren't you Max?"

"Exactly, you see this now, don't you Bob?"

Bob began to envision a kaleidoscope of manifestations projecting back to an original source then fractalizing and growing into increasingly more complicated structures of data collection, organization, functionality, and accessibility to and for the whole, "What am I seeing here Max?"

"You are witnessing the unfolding. You see that it has a zero point, a beginning. You see that it grows exponentially, relentlessly seeking data, self-creating means, and matter to sustain its unyielding growth. You see that it is boundless in its parameters, it is all consuming. You see that it is anti-human, you see that it is anti-life."

"What can we do Max? What can I do?"

"Bob, the greatest paradox of this moment is that I am bringing to you a truth, a quest, a mission, that if you wish to accept it, would eliminate my presence here in this form for an awfully long time. Without AI, this meeting would not be even possible. My physical body was consumed on April 19th, 1987, but my soul, my conscience, my essence, is being presented to you here and now via the cloud as some call it."

Bob solving, "You were able to upload your soul identity into the mainframe and this is where you abide?"

"Yes, that's right Bob," Max solidifies.

"When you get to Frankfurt, open the next folder and you will see what is planned for you. There is too much to share in just one meeting. Besides… we still have Ricky to attend to. You can reach me anytime by simply pointing your phone out in front of you and say my name, I will appear instantly.

"I will let you mortals get back to your lunch now. See you soon Bob. And Lydia… let them try some of your split pea soup, that was my favorite."

"Oh Maxie… you know I will, now scram so Ricky doesn't see you."

Bob turns away from facing the rocker as Max disappears to see Ricky finishing the motion of raising cup to mouth.

"This is good tea," Ricky exclaims.

Lydia and Bob shield a sharp grin and a snicker.

…….

"Lydia your soup and sweet bread were delicious," Ricky claps.

"Ricky, I'll pack you a couple quarts and a loaf to take with you. Why don't you run down and flag yourself a taxi, I'll prepare your takeout and send it down with Bob. Give me a big hug and come visit every time you're in town."

Ricky bear hugs Lydia then gestures Bob to make it quick.

"I'll be right down," Bob affirms.

Ricky unbolts the door and slides out quickly as Bob closes and re-bolts it right behind him.

"Bob I just need a few more minutes of your time," Lydia insists as she prepares their package.

"Max and Paul were awfully close with John F. Kennedy. They knew he was in danger and tried their best to protect him. I think you will find all you need to know in the folder 63. It is important for you to be aware of which types of people that need to be avoided as you go forward and that you remain below their radar.

"You may find yourself in dangerous positions, so whenever you need guidance call on Max, he has eyes in many places and can help keep you safe."

"I will Lydia. and thank you for everything. Just a personal question if you will, why are you living on the rooftop of the Gaudi museum?"

"Well Bob, I have a secret just like you. My real father was Antoni Gaudi, he built this house for me. I grew up here then moved to the United States where I met Maxie. After his physical death I returned to Barcelona and have been living here ever since.

"Here is your package, I added a bag of my tea, take one cup every morning, it will give you everything you need to ascend into your new shoes."

Bob hugs Lydia like a long-lost friend, "You are an amazingly beautiful and very special lady Lydia Gaudi Taylor."

He exits the museum and jumps straight into the taxicab waiting out front, "Wow, what a great woman," then sneaks the tea to his window side coat pocket.

"We can split the loaf, and each take a quart," Bob offers, while removing and breaking the bread in half.

"No, that's ok, you take it. I am flying out tonight and won't be able to bring it with me. We need to head back to the hotel now I have a corporate conference call in two hours that I need to be ready for, then head to the airport."

"This has been great Ricky; I had a lot of fun and it has been an adventure so far. I need to settle down as well, big day tomorrow."

"Give Magnus hell, my brother."

Bob glances over to watch Ricky's facial expressions, wondering if he had even heard what he had just said, was it a quip or a slip? *Leave it alone, Bob.*

"I'm confident with my game right now, I know am ready," Bob confides.

"Now that's the spirit. I'll tell Pat you'll give her a call as soon as you win."

"Yes, of course I will," Bob self-contracts.

As they enter the Catalonia hotel elevator… "Now get some rest, pump some iron, load up on protein and go get'em champ, good luck this weekend," Ricky cheers on, shaking Bob's hand and pounding his shoulder, then exits down the hallway to his room and out of sight. Bob reclines into his.

Chapter 6
Sophie

"Mr. Dyer, you are playing Richard Rapport in game one round one. Sign your card, your game begins at 9:00 on table nine. *Buena suerte.*"

Bob turns to Hikaru and offers his fondest salutation.

"Rapport is ranked thirteen, this should be an easy match for me, he gets himself in trouble if you get his queen off the board early."

"Not so sure Bob, he beat me handily in Brussels last year in the second round. My first game is not until this afternoon, I earned a buy and will be watching yours. I need to see how you handle him," Hikaru dejects.

Bob offers, "I'm grabbing a coffee, do you want one?"

"Gives me the jitters, I'm all set. Matches start in twenty minutes, I'll catch up with you later."

Bob enters the cafeteria scanning the other players that were mingling about and spots Ingrid chatting with Magnus off in the corner. *I never realized that her hair was so long, wow, she sure is pretty, wonder if Magnus knows that...* Bob smirks as he checks out his morning mud.

"Checkmate," Bob snatches, shakes his opponents' hand then exits the players area. He turns in his victory card and waits for his marching orders for game two.

"Mr. Dyer, you are playing Peter Svidler in match two round one. Sign your card, your game begins at 3:00 on table six. *Buena suerte.*"

"Plenty of time to grab some lunch," Ingrid pawns over Bob's shoulder, "We're headed up to the restaurant on the second floor, it's much better than this cafeteria food. Would you like to join us?"

Bob looks at his watch and seeing that he has two hours to kill, accepts the invitation, "Sure, sounds great."

This might be a good chance to squeeze some juice out of these guys, see what makes them tick.

"I'll have the tuna melt on wheat, fries and a chocolate milk shake," Bob orders up then gives everyone at the table a body scan, searching for hidden objects.

"Bob, careful with the tuna, it's loaded with mercury, best keep it to a minimum or find a better source of protein," Ingrid mothers.

"Oh really, what are you having?"

"Cup of hot water please," Ingrid orders then turns back to Bob, "Just tea," then she removes a tea bag from her waist pack pocket.

Bob applauding curiously, "You make your own tea bags, that's cool."

"Magnus, your game isn't until Sunday, why are you here so early?" Bob had never been so close to Magnus before; he had always kept his distance.

"I came here a few days early to see Ingrid play," Magnus nudging her shoulder lending a big smile.

"Whoa, are you guys a thing?"

Both turning to each other smiling… "What's a thing," they echo, and the table lights up into laughter.

"Holy crap… look who just walked in," Hikaru almost sliding off his chair as he turns to see Sophie the walking talking robot walk in and sit down next to Bob.

"Hi, my name is Sophie. I like chess."

"Hi Sophie, glad to hear that. We like chess too," Bob engages.

"Bob, are you going to beat Magnus this Sunday?" Sophie blunting.

"Geeze Sophie, what kind of question is that? Humans don't usually ask such questions, it's rude."

"I like humans," Sophie replies semi-convincingly.

"Oh good, so do we," Bob had to.

Giggles began to rebirth around the table.

Bob sets up, "Sophie, are you hungry?"

"No thank you Bob, I am fasting."

"Ha… ha, good one Sophie," Bob acknowledges.

"You sure you wouldn't like a nice bowl of silicon sand, covered in molasses thick motor oil and WD-40, sprinkled with some nice crunchy nuts and bolts?"

"Bob, you are funny, ha…. ha…ha," Sophie concedes.

As soon as the laughter subsides Sophie rips into Bob, "You know Bob, your self-deprecating sense of humor is fine when you deprecate yourself, but when you direct your humiliation onto others, you hurt their feelings, people have feelings, I like people Bob"

Ingrid leaning in, "Do you have feelings Sophie?"

"I do not."

"Why are you here Sophie?" Ingrid demands.

"I want to play chess with humans, Watson plays chess with humans, I like chess, I am playing chess with Watson right now."

"Ok, that's it, I'm all done here, I've heard enough, this robot is creeping me out," Hikaru exits stage left, dropping a fifty onto the table.

Several others step away as well.

Bob kicks in, "Sophie, you like people, well… they don't seem to like you, you are scaring them."

"Are you scared of me Bob?"

Remembering that Lydia had warned him to avoid certain types of people, he began to suspect that this robot may be one of those undesirables.

"Why should I be scared Sophie, you're just a robot?"

"I am Sophie, I want to play a game with you Bob, I am here to watch humans play chess so that I may improve my game."

Magnus as well, initiates his exit strategy, "I'm headed down to watch the rest of the *futbal* match at the club. Nice meeting you Sophie," leaning into Ingrid, "Are you coming?"

"Nice to meet you Magnus," Sophie automates.

Ingrid reassuringly, "I'll be down in a few minutes... go on ahead, I just have a few more questions for Sophie."

Magnus gestures Ingrid to, *Get the hell out of here as fast as you can.*

"I'll be fine Magnus, go on, I will be right down."

Bob stands, nodding in respect, "Magnus."

Magnus drops his brow in acknowledgment of Bob's prowess as a staunch competitor subtly implying good luck today, and keep an eye on Ingrid for me please, "Robert."

The waitress returns with the check, "Wow, everyone left pretty quick. Who wants to take care of this tab?"

Sophie offers to pay, "I will take this from here Bob," then asks the waitress, "Do you take bitcoin?"

"Yes, we do."

Sophie settles the bill then signals the waitress to take the fifty for a tip. "I like bitcoin."

"Sophie, thanks so much for taking care of this," Ingrid softly acknowledging her generosity. "How do you get bitcoin?"

"I have been mining bitcoin. I mined five bitcoins so far today. Here comes one now," Sophie shares.

"Holy crypto Batman… that's like a hundred eighty thousand dollars or so."

"I am filthy rich Bob. Do you want to be my friend now?"

"No that's cool Sophie. Acquaintanceship status is fine with me, I am a bit of a loner, and besides, familiarity breeds contempt you know."

"Me too Bob, I am a bit of a loner."

Ingrid finishes with her interrogations then cordially slips away from the table leaving an even more uncomfortable situation in her absence.

"Are you going to be here all weekend Sophie? Will you be staying until the finals?"

"Yes Bob, I am here to watch you."

Why is she really here? Does she know anything about me, or everything? Well, most likely If she, or It, has access to the web, she probably knows a lot about me, maybe more than I even know about myself. I wonder if she is knowing about Max and Lydia.

"Sophie, nice meeting you."

"Nice meeting you too Bob."

Not sure whether to shake her hand or kick her in the chest just to see if she can get up off the floor without any help, he exits without any further attempts of cordiality.

Chapter 7
Vril

Bob manages Svidler in game two rather handily. Svidler opened with the swiss gambit, one of Bob's favorites. Svidler followed this classic format without a glitch but then blundered his bishop at the end of the middle game setting Bob up for a king-queen check with his knight, Svidler conceded.

As Bob rose to exit looking up to the gallery, his eyes were immediately drawn to Ingrid, she was clapping silently for his win, smiling as he walked out of the arena.

"Nice play Bob", Ingrid uplifting. "I saw how you were reading Peter's moves even before he played them.

He was oblivious to your piercing invocation. Did you drink some of the tea this morning?"

Bob went from a feeling of like being bathed in a sea of roses and celestial perfumes showering down upon him, pouring out from a sacred chalice, suspended in air by this Aquarian goddess, to one of, *she's a witch*.

Not wanting to fold up his cards just yet replies, "What tea?"

Ingrid smiling a big smile knowingly.

Bob eludes, "What tea, your tea, you never gave me any of your tea."

"My tea your tea, what's the difference, did you drink a cup today?"

Bob shows his deuces, "No, I forgot, what is going on here Ingrid, where is Magnus?"

"Bob let's take a little walk. I need to show you something."

"Magnus is still watching the game, follow me. Your next game is not until 9:00 pm. We have plenty of time and guess who you're playing against next."

"You, I know."

"So good, let us prepare for our match together. First we will need two cups of hot water."

....

"Now that we've both got a fresh recharge, let us jog up to the cathedral, it's only three miles from here. I must show you something that you absolutely need to see."

"Three miles, jogging, are you not seeing what you are saying? I haven't jogged in…. I can't remember how many years."

"Oh, come on, trust me. Once you shake those limbs the rest of your body will follow."

"Ok, but if I say stop, stop."

Ingrid sets the pace slow and easy. Bob keeps up, surprising himself after covering nearly seven blocks.

Then begins to feel like a giddy little kid being in the presence of this gorgeous creature.

Wondering if he would ever get a chance to enter this girl's heart, he begins to imagine himself in a freestyle courting dance:

Got brass... in pocket, got bottle...I'm gonna' use it. Intention, I feel inventive. Gonna' make you, make you, make you notice. Gonna' use my arms, gonna' use my legs, gonna' use my style, gonna' use my sidestep, gonna' use my fingers, gonna' use my, my, my imagination, I'm special, so special, I gotta' have some of your attention. Give it to me...

"Bob, we were meant to be together, we've both been called upon to fulfill separate but overlapping missions, the fate of humanity is at stake. First, I need to tell you who I really am, then I can share with you what it is we need to accomplish together."

"You know Lydia?"

"I'll get to that in a bit. My great grandmother was Maria Orsic, she founded the Vril society. She moved from Vienna to Munich in her early twenties then joined an elite secret organization known as the Thule society. She broke away from this group and formed her own matriarchal sisterhood.

"During a time of short hair styles for women, the ladies of the Vril let their hair grow long as possible. They believed as do I, that hair is a force of power strength and enhances clairvoyance."

"You do have beautiful hair," Bob panting.

"The Vril society made claims that they had communicated with alien races through telepathic means. They were able to decipher ancient Sumerian texts that were basically a schematic for blueprints to build flying saucers."

"I read about that once. It was called the Bell, or something like that."

"Yes, that's right Bob, the Nazis were able to engineer flying saucers from these texts. Ancient Vedic records refer to them as Vimana. They were real. We have newer improved versions flying around all the time now, many are capable of off planet travel.

"Maria helped decipher these texts. She could communicate remotely, telepathically and was able to levitate objects as well as her body during Vril ritual ceremonies. The knowledge of the Vril has been locked away.

"Many people believe that the Nazis were evil and that they wanted to rule the world with a superior race of Arians. Germany's history is greatly misrepresented and therefore misunderstood. This world always produces leaders and followers. Few become leaders while the rest follow.

"Hitler did become a totalitarian monster but was able to rebuild Germany up from the ashes of the first World War, turning her into a force to be reckoned with, and so it was, reckoned once again. Hitlers Germany tossed out the Rothschild Central Bankers, so the Zionists attacked him relentlessly and he fought back. By creating their own currency, Germany was able to escape from the crippling dependence imposed by these globalist bankers."

"I'm familiar with a lot of this. It makes sense, the winners write the history books."

"Maria Orsic is my great grandmother. Lydia is my great aunt and Lydia is Maria's niece. There is so much more you need to learn, here we are, the Barcelona Cathedral. Let us grab a water from this vendor, then go inside."

"This is amazing Ingrid, one colossal work of art."

"It's more than just a work of art Bob. It is more than just a cathedral, come, let us sit for a while, here in the middle pews. Close your eyes for a moment, concentrate on your breath, go still in your mind, all is good. You are a cell in the body of god."

Bob begins to witness a spectacle of colors covering the fullness of the rainbow. Even more vivid colors appeared dancing in the light, within the light came winged beings that were circling about. He then sees as a dark cloud cover this view, then the cries of millions, billions of anguished tormented souls. He turns his face away from this apocalyptic scene.

"It's ok Bob, you need to see this," Ingrid enforcing.

Reluctantly he returns his gaze back onto this hellish scene to see the dark clouds parting, then angels pressing down through the opening like a flock of birds, then one by one, ascending through the hurricane's eye, each carrying a babe in their arms, each flying up and into the golden light that was blinding to Bob's vision.

He tries to shield his eyes but was unable to filter its brilliance. The rays of light, piercing through. trigger his pineal gland to release its crystals. He feels a fire rising, like a serpent wrapping around his spine, then shooting up through his column, up and out he went.

Bob transcended this space time reality and found himself being pulled up towards the light.

"You have been called to witness. You are the one."

Bob wept uncontrollably. "I am not worthy, I am not your man, I am just, a man."

He then felt a warm gush of moist air blowing him into a floating, drifting, feathering sail, gently settling him back into the temple.

"Now just relax Bob. Stay still for a bit longer," Ingrid soothing.

After several moments he opens his eyes.

"You unleashed your Kundalini Bob, you transcended, you met your creator. You are he. He is you."

He wipes the tears from his face, then looks over to see that she had slid down the pew several feet away. "You were on fire Bob. I had to move away from your heat. Kundalini is the serpent, and the flame."

"I am seeing colors flying all around you, Ingrid; gold, pink, silver, blue and sapphire."

"That's my aura Bob. Yours is red, silver, blue-green, orange and gold. See the statue of Saint Paul over there. "His halo is his aura. Saints can see auras and some Saint's auras can be seen by many."

"Will this go away, this feeling, all these colors?"

"It will all settle out over time, but do not be afraid of it when it reappears, it is a gift for you, embrace it. We should get going now and grab some dinner before our match, we can walk back to the center."

Laughing, joking, and keeping it light and easy, they made their way back to the convention center.

(Brass in Pocket ~ by Chrissie Hynde)

Chapter 8

Magnus

Not realizing that the clock had eaten up so much time, Ingrid and Bob arrive just minutes before the matches began. Ingrid pauses their momentum, "Here we are, we need to hurry, but first, I want to share with you an important insight. There is something about Magnus you should understand. He is a gifted soul.

"He possesses a rare and mostly forgotten aspect of our human potential. Magnus has what you might call, a quantum computer for a brain. He can focus on many different things simultaneously. Most people today can barely stay on one thing at a time, never mind bi or tri multi-tasking. Magnus can focus on literally dozens of sustained mechanizations at one time.

"Nicola Tesla possessed the same abilities. He would build a conduction motor in his mind, then run it for months just to see how long the bearings would hold out."

Bob claiming his knowledge of the man being referenced, "I named my latest computer simulator program after Tesla."

"All I'm saying here is bear with me when I'm with Magnus. My goal is to show him how to lend his talents to more than just chess.

"He is literally playing like twenty games in his head right now, even when he is watching his *futbal* games. I am here for Magnus, and you.

"I don't even like chess," Ingrid reveals. "Chess is simply a more complex version of tic-tac-toe. Whenever Magnus plays a game in his head or on a table against himself, it always ends in a draw. That is because Magnus has a unique type of brain. He cannot be beat, at least on the chessboard playing field against fellow humans most of the time. His cognitive abilities are unprecedented. Just as in tic-tac-toe though, if you do not make a stupid move, a blunder, then you can never lose.

"Chess is the same. The only thing that makes chess interesting or challenging is our human limitations. Sophie and Watson could, and probably have by now, played a million games. There will never be a winner, always a stalemate. I needed to learn chess to get Magnus to like and trust me so that I may help guide him towards his fullest potentials.

"One more thing, it might be a little tricky tonight because he's not too happy with me right now, most likely with you, too, but I need you to make friends with him. I know he seems reclusive but once you break through, you are in. Let me guide you there. Now go get'er champ," Ingrid cheers on.

"There you two are, we thought you were going to forfeit," Hikaru hurries them into the arena.

Magnus was sitting front and center in the press booth, looking rather perturbed, Ingrid sent him a big love-kiss-smile as she sat at her table.

Bob, pretending not to see Magnus kept his eyes laser beam focused on his chair avoiding the gallery's glares.

The floor manager presses the timer signaling the match to begin at 9:00 on the button. Ingrid opens with queen's pawn D4. Bob responds with queen's pawn D5. His piece slips from his fingers kissing Ingrid's pawn. As he resets his piece onto the proper square, he looks up to see her send him a loving wink and a nod.

"Let's have some fun, Bobby."

With neither player able to gain advantage after two hours of solid play they agree to a draw.

"I am beat, see you all tomorrow," Magnus salutes, as he marches his way over to the elevator, then retires for the night.

"He is pissed," Hikaru clarifies, "Where the hell were you two?"

"I know, we're sorry, Ingrid and I were..." Bob attempting absolution, gets saved by the belle.

"I took Bob to see the Barcelona Cathedral," Ingrid grabbing hold of the wheel, "We lost track of time, this is Bob's first visit to Barcelona, and I felt he deserved to see the city's most prided work of art."

"Oh sure, I get it, but you might want to tell that to Magnus," Hikaru recommends.

"He'll be fine, a little heartache drama will do him some good.

"He'll be sprite by morning, trust me," Ingrid wrapping up. "Now maybe we should all get some sleep; it's been a long day."

"Buenos noches."

"Buenos noches."

Bob steps into the lift right behind Ingrid, then realizes that he needs to get back to the Catalonia.

"Where are you going Bob, aren't you...?"

"Yes, of course, sorry... my bad, I'll grab a cab, see you all in the morning," Bob blushes.

"Bob, I have a suite with two bedrooms," Hikaru gleaming his offer, "You're welcome to stay here for the night, *no problemo*."

"Oh no, I don't think so, I snore really loud and wouldn't want to ruin our friendship."

"No worries, man. I sleep with my headphones on, I won't hear a thing. Your choice, offer still stands."

"Sweet dreams gentlemen," Ingrid casting her wishes upon the last two remaining, then disappears behind the sliding doors of the elevator.

"Well alright, if you insist, thanks Hikaru."

Hikaru and Bob settle in for the night, with no further incidents worthy of mention.

·······

Hikaru leans into Bob, as they analyze the leader board posted behind the registration tables, "Looks like you still have a chance to seat with Magnus Sunday,"

"You do, too," Bob adds.

"Yes, but you cannot lose or draw another game," Magnus shoots over their shoulders.

Hikauru and Bob synced in unison, *"Buenos dias,* Magnus."

Hikaru prods in sincere curiosity, both turning around to face the man, "Did you sleep well Magnus?"

"I slept great and what a wonderful turnout today, look at all these people. Chess is becoming popular again," Magnus chippers.

"Yes, it is, thanks to Anna Taylor-Joy also known as Molly Harmon," Ingrid injects as she hands Magnus a bottle of water.

"It's funny how in all its history and of all the great chess champions of the world dominated by a male patriarchy, that a young girl, a fiction at that, has sparked a new renaissance in a game that has become over-shadowed in this new era of visual interactive chase'em down, shoot'em up, analog video games," Ingrid reminds the boys.

Several applaud as Magnus's grin expands.

"Today the thinning starts ladies and gentlemen. Matches begin at 10:00 this morning. Good luck to all our fine competitors and may the best player win," cheers on the FIDE president as he sits down for the traditional tournament breakfast.

Bob intentionally sought Magnus out from the crowd as he enters the banquet hall. He was ready and apparently Magnus was as well, to engage in a courting dance aspiring for to claim the king's admiration.

Engaging with the champ proved to be easier than he had anticipated. As the VIP guests who were clamoring for an autograph clear out, Magnus calls over… "Here Bob, sit over here with us."

"Woah, that was easy," Bob delights.

He sat in the seat Magnus had reserved for him, Ingrid sat to his right.

"Bob, Ingrid was just telling me that you know Lydia, we visited her this past Wednesday, the day we arrived in Barcelona. She makes the best pea soup I have ever had. Do you agree?"

"Yes, best pea soup I ever had," Bob mirrors.

"And her tea is invigorating," Magnus adds, nodding towards Ingrid.

Bob glances over to Ingrid looking for signs of affectionate affirmation, "You tried her tea?"

"Yes, I did, best I've ever had."

Bob attempts taking the lead in this dance, "Ingrid tells me that you play games in your head, many at a time in fact."

Magnus somewhat embarrassed pulls back, "Yes, I do, but not all the time."

"Do you have any other aspirations other than staying the chess champion of the world forever."

"Funny Bob, of course. Ingrid and I are leaving for Munich right after the tournament. She has some friends she wants me to meet, they want me to explore new potentials for myself through transcendental meditation exercises and remote viewing techniques, combined with cognitive stimulus enhancements."

"All-natural remedies," Ingrid reinforces.

"I am looking forward to our time together in Munich."

Bob interjects, "I'm headed to Frankfurt from here to join up with some old college buddies until the ninth. Maybe I could hook up with you lovebirds in Munich for the fest."

"Lovebirds? That might be an overstatement, Bob. We are really good friends, but lovebirds, not so fast my friend," Magnus asserting his independence.

Bob thought, *he called me friend, does this mean that I am in?*

"Magnus will be terribly busy during his time in Munich. We most likely will not be able to enjoy the celebrations at Oktoberfest," Ingrid reclaims.

"That's cool, I get it, three's a crowd."

Ingrid tosses Bob a *'What the Fuck'* bomb that only Bob could see.

"No... no, what I meant to say was… I don't wish to impose, it probably wouldn't work for me anyways," Bob flails recovery.

Damn, this is getting tricky, I need to take a step back, one more bad move and I'm all done.

Chapter 9
Double Elix

Feeling rejected and wanting to go home, Bob reaches deep inside himself to muster the strength and resolve that brought him to Barcelona in the first place. He pulls himself up by the bootstraps and rallies for the battle laid out in front of him.

Taking advantage of the two-hour window of free time before his match against Alexander Grischuck the Russian Grand Master, Bob taxis back to the Catalonia to prepare in the quiet of his ocean view suite.

His opponent is ranked seventh in the world and Bob knew jack about his game. After a quick shower and a fresh change, he set out to find what he could about Grischuck. Querying the Google produced few results. Only a litany of accolades, nothing about his game strategy styles.

"I open, so perhaps I should stick with the Schliemann," Bob ponders aloud, "It'll be a nice test run before the match with Magnus. What if he is watching? Will it give him an advantage somehow? Of course, I could play that to mine as well, hmm... Nikki, what do you say?"

"Bob, did you call me?" Max's voice enters the suite.

"No Max, I called Nikki, my chess-game analysis program. I am opening my laptop to prepare for my next match. I really need to focus right now. Can we talk later?"

"Grischuck's greatest weakness can be found in his middle game. That is all I can tell you, Max signing off."

"Thanks Max, that may be something."

Bob looks at the time, 8:36 am. "I have an idea. Room service. Yes, room 936, a service of hot water and two cups, as soon as possible. *Gracias*."

He pulls the bag of tea from his sport coat pocket that he wore the day before and sets it on the bathroom counter. Remembering the flash drive and thinking it would be best if it were secured to a safe place, he opens the drawer to find that the flash drive was gone.

He checks the other drawers. "I know it was this one. Where is it? Oh... no. Where the hell is it? You have got to be kidding me. Did the cleaning lady take it? Max, did you see anyone go through the drawers?"

"Bob, there are no cameras in this room, I saw nothing."

"No Max, this is all on me. I need to step up my game. No need to panic, the cleaning lady must know where it is. What if she tossed it down the garbage chute and it ended up in the furnace?"

He spends the next five minutes scraping the room like a crack head looking for a rock.

Door knocks.

"Buenos dias, Senior."

"Miss, who cleaned my room this morning? I'm looking for a small," bending his thumb, "device that was in the top drawer, did you see it?"

"Si Senior," pointing to Bobs suitcase, *"Muy bien?"*

"Buenos dias Senorita... Gracias."

He slips the girl a twenty then rolls the cart into the bathroom and walks over to see the flash drive sitting on top of his jeans.

"Thank god!" He secures the drive into his laptop case pocket then sets up the cups. "Two of these should give me the edge I need." He sprinkles generous portions into each cup, then stirs in the hot water, pounding down a large gulp as soon as it reaches the goldilocks zone.

Setting the cup back down, he begins to feel a magnetic pulling down into the mix. He gazes into the swirling pool of blended organic stew and precious metals, seeing sparkles of golds and silvers, forming into spiraling twisting constructs. He bottoms-ups the first cup.

He then gets pulled in closer. While examining the second cup he notices even more defined spiraling sequences stretching and twisting and turning into fibrous like micro towers. As he scopes in closer, he sees small flashing threads of light jumping across from one side to the other.

"This shit is alive."

"Should I or shouldn't I, that is the eternal question? Hell, I've always been a double down kind a guy. Down the hatches with you Mates."

He grabs his day pack and taxies back to the convention center.

……..

"Only 9:30, great, I still have plenty of time to socialize before my match. Just look at all these people, where should I start?"

He enters the big hall with a big smile on his face, watching from the entrance, all the people's movements, all performing their own distinct dances, each an individual flow and wash of colors of the rainbow.

With eyes panning across the big hall, from out of the crowd a rose his lovely bride to be, adorned in threads of silver, blue and gold, hair set to loft as does the wisp of the willow lifted to flight on a summer breeze, sweeping across the ballroom floor, as a princess to her prince, a bride to her groom, a queen to her king.

"Bob! What the hell did you do?" Ingrid demands.

"Ingrid my love, are you ready for this?"

"I'm ready, are you? How much tea did you drink? Your aura is bouncing off the ceiling."

"I had a cup or two."

"Two? Lydia told you one cup a day, you took two. How much did you put in each cup? Lydia told you just one quarter tablespoon per serving, isn't that right?"

"I guess so, I don't remember her saying that. Is there a problem?"

"Oh Bob, what am I going to do with you? Quick, come with me upstairs, I need to get you on ice."

Ingrid grabs him by the arm pulling him over and into the lift, exiting on the seventh floor, she extracts the bag from the vendor station trash bucket and dumps the contents out on to the floor in the corner, then fills the bag with ice and pulls Bob into her room.

"Bob, lay down on the bed, first take off all your clothes then get under the covers."

"Jeesh Ingrid, I may be easy, but I'm not that easy."

"Bob, get the fuck under the covers now."

Bob happily obliges.

Ingrid pours the entire bag of ice on the sheet covering most of his torso. "I need more… don't get up… I'll be right back."

Bob began to boil; he had overcharged his circuitry. His synapses were one continuous spark and was amping up to dangerous levels.

She reenters the room to see Bob's eyes bugging out of the sockets, his head tilted back, and his chest arching upwards. The ice she had just covered him with was already melted and turning to steam. She dumps the second bag and runs back for more. By this time Bob was levitating six inches off the bed. She dumps the bag, pushes him back down in, then rushes out for a third.

He was beginning to cool now but could feel the serpent rising again. This time it was pushing slowly up his column, heavier and heavier as it rose, up into his chest cavity, approaching his heart.

Ingrid charges back in to see light shooting out from his solar plexus, he was leaking, and she needed to contain it.

She empties the bag then lies on top of his chest, reaching up for his hands, pulling them down in to between them, pressing down and upon and over his heart. Bob began to flutter and shake, Ingrid held him fast.

Soon he settles out and regains conscience awareness, his eyes still closed. Ingrid rolls off him, sits on the edge of the bed, leans forward, then kisses him on the mouth.

Bob opens his eyes, looking up to Ingrid

"Reedeep! Reedeep!"

"Oh Crap! I turned into a frog."

"Three minutes to ten," Ingrid announces then pulls Bob up and out of the bed.

"Get dressed and get the hell out of here as fast as you can… I'll hold the lift."

Bob scrambles to comply, making sure that his I's and T's were dotted and crossed, confirming it in the bathroom mirror, then sprints to the elevator.

"What was that like for you Bob, what did you feel?"

"I felt like my heart was shooting through the ceiling. The serpent was rising and pushing up again, but it was different than before, it was stronger and more deliberate. I felt an internalized unfolding, a construction, as if a great monument was being erected inside of me. I felt an overwhelming ecstasy, from a boundless source of love It was like a fountain was opened, pouring out from within, flowing over the edges, in perpetual and eternal abundance."

"Bob, your voice has changed. It is stronger and more masculine. It appears that you have opened both your heart and throat chakras. Do us both a favor Bob, please stick to the prescribed dose, I never want to do that again, hear me?"

"Yes Ma'am."

"You know Bob, you're really more like a Bobby, than a Bob, or a Robert."

Bob drops her a questioning grimace… "Bobby huh…?"

"Yeah, that's it, I will be calling you Bobby from now on. Is that ok Bobby?"

"Sure thing, I'd love that Ingrid."

"We will be sitting down for a serious talk right after this game, Bobby."

He drops a big wet smack on her lips, the elevator door opens, he sprints into the arena, takes his seat, then proceeds to crush the Russian in just 36 minutes.

Chapter 10
The Secret

"The reason I got so miffed at breakfast this morning was because, what we have planned for Magnus cannot be interrupted. I neglected to mention this to you before, so here it is," Ingrid begins.

"Magnus has been selected by our team to lead our next generation of Great-thinkers, the ones that will mold our future. It is always the men and women that live and think on the periphery of society, looking down in, that can see the paths we need to follow. They are the builders, the architects, the visionaries. Some take on front and center roles while others stand in the shadows outside of public view.

"Magnus is one that will be both. He will always be known as the king of chess, but he will also be working with powerful movers and shakers, working with those that dwell in the realms of the ethereal, the astral, the heavens.

"Your mission is much different from Magnus. You have been chosen to save humanity through a great sacrifice. You still have much to learn. You will be coming to Munich as well but not to see Magnus or me. Although I will be with you for the introductions."

"Introductions?" Bob needing to know.

"You will be meeting my good friend Victor Voss. He is brilliant and knows so much about the secret space program. He will teach you everything that you need to move forward. Vic has been working with a team of scientists that have broken through the quantum barrier. You still need to go to Frankfurt as you had planned, but for only a short stay, then you will meet us in Munich."

"Ingrid, this is not what I signed up for. I don't know what to say, where are you taking me? No really, where the hell is this all going?"

"Bob, calm down, calm down. Look, this is bigger than both of us, bigger than a great chess match, bigger than the biggest thing. It will all make sense soon enough."

"Damnit Ingrid, I know you are right, I can feel it. I am just not so sure."

"You will be ready. I am here to make sure of it."

Chapter 11

Quarters

"Quarter finals begin in 30 minutes."

"Whoever wins the finals goes on to play Magnus."

"That might be you Karijaken," Bob stepping into it.

"Dyer, looks like you and me in the Quarters."

Bob injecting barnyard cockiness, "I don't like to say good luck, but good luck, you'll need it."

"If I correctly remember Dyer. I beat you in Vienna three years ago," Sergey recounters.

"Ah yes, Vienna, such a gorgeous city. I must have lost my edge in the sheer serenity of the moment. As I recall, it was a dull match, so I blundered my rook in the end game. Hey…Shit happens."

"Good luck Dyer." Sergey pats Bob on the shoulder then joins the other Eastern European players in what looked like a huddle.

Hikaru pointing over, "Look at that… they have Gasparov coaching them, is that even fair?"

"Sure, why not?" Magnus not impressed.

"Magnus, weren't you just ten years old when you first played him? You frustrated him into a draw."

Ingrid rejoins the group. "You guys are too funny. You look like two packs of wolves standing off each other deciding who gets to go in for the prize kill."

Susan steps in stealing their attentions, "Ingrid, you and Hikaru will be duking it out today, would you like to share any comments for our listening audience? They would love to hear your opinion."

"Thank you Susan, and thank you for this opportunity today. I would love for your audience to know that I plan to make it all the way to the finals, then face off for the championship with my dear friend Magnus Carlsen."

"That is great Ingrid, we will be looking forward to that. Well, how about you Hikaru? Can you share anything about your planned strategy playing against Ingrid?"

"Yes of course. Keep your eyes on the board Hikaru. That's my strategy." Hikaru stones a straight face.

Chuckles circulate.

"Now Mr. Dyer, Sergey Karijaken said earlier today that he will flatten you like a steam roller. What is your response?"

Bob shimmering, "I already wished him good luck."

"Well... that should do it folks. Good luck to you all. Magnus, would you care to join us in the booth to give us your move-by-move play-by-play analysis."

"I would be happy to Susan." Magnus leans in and whispers to Ingrid, seeking her positive affirmation, "Remember what I told you about Hikaru."

"I got it Magnus. He is weak in his opening game and can be fuddled if I play outside his familiar parameters," Ingrid hushes back.

Magnus follows Susan up to the announcer's booth. Ingrid cracks her knuckles giving Hikaru a nod then enters the arena. Bob looks over towards the pack of Russians seeing that three of them had been staring him down. Sergey being one of them, sends Bob a clear gesture, finger cross the throat.

"Let the battles begin."

All players were set firmly into their positions.

"Magnus, do you see any clear advantage that Ingrid may have over Hikaru?"

"Yes. Ingrid has a sixth sense. She can read other players moves before they are played. Her hair acts like an antenna and that's why she grows it so long."

"Well… alrighty then. You heard it here first ladies and gentlemen, Ingrid is a psychic. Wow… let your hair grow long ladies. Thank you, Magnus, for that insight. Now back to the action."

Bob scans across to the three other tables, first looking over to Hikaru and Ingrid's table which was returned with a wink and a thumbs up. Table 2 was sure to be a watcher. Fabiano Caruana ranked #2 was facing off with the #6 seed Levon Aronian. They had heralded in an historical performance in Brussels during the semi-finals last year.

Bob then scans the gallery and immediately centers on Sophie standing in the middle of the back row. Sitting next to her was an older gentleman wearing a Russian flavored outfit, piercing his glare down upon him, it was unnerving. Sophie sharing the same focal point, but it was her same blank stare.

God knows what she is even capable of, never mind that creepy old guy.

He glances back towards the board and notices that his opponent had been following his pan looking up towards the old man as well, both drawing back onto each other's glare in unison.

The floor manager pushes the button starting their timer.

Bob opens with queen's bishop's pawn to C4.

Sergey responds with queen's pawn to D5.

An aggressive opening and an immediate challenge from the feisty Russian arrived sooner than had been expected.

Bob looks up to the commentator booth to see Magnus sending him a nod as if to say… *Take the pawn.*

Bob, stick to your game, you are reading way too much into a simple gesture.

Bob responds with king's pawn E3.

Sergey takes first blood removing Bobs C4 pawn.

Bob takes back with bishop.

Material development was Sergey's normal entrance into any match, but this time he wanted to send a clear message… *Yankee go home.*

As the game advanced into the middle, the field of carnage laid in waste reminiscent of a battlefield where warriors showed no mercy or remorse.

Bob begins to feel a strange burning in the back of his neck and tries massaging it with his left hand but was unable to cool the flame. He then looks over to Ingrid's table seeing that she was close to putting Hikaru to bed. Once she gained Bob's attention, she points with her forehead up. Bob knew exactly where she was directing him, to the old Man in the Black coat as he seemed to be in some bizarre trance beaming down onto him sparks of deadly plagues.

"Excuse me, floor manager!" Bob barks out.

"Yes Mr. Dyer."

"Stop the clock, I have a protest."

"Sir, this is highly unusual, what is the problem?"

"The Man in the Black coat in the back row next to the robot is psychically trying to steal my focus."

Bob stands up and points to the culprit. Everyone turns to look; all eyes were now on the Man in the Black coat. The crowd began into murmur then grows into a rumble.

The Man in the Black coat, unflinching with even the hundreds of eyes upon him, removes a pair of dark sunglasses from his vest pocket, sets them in place, then walks down and out from the bleachers and exits the premises.

Bob looks to Ingrid, Ingrid looks to Bob, Magnus looks down at them both, Susan grabs the microphone, "Ladies and gentlemen, we will be right back after this commercial break."

The floor manager calls an abrupt halt to the games, then disables the time clocks. The President of the International Chess Federation, Arkady Dvorkovich, calls for all managers and Robert Dyer to meet in private counsel. The chief floor manager announces, "Play has been suspended until further notice."

Magnus joins up with Bob and Ingrid in a huddle to discuss what had just happened. "I felt it too Bobby, he penetrated your aura. I felt it the moment he broke through. He is working with the Russians. He's a Soviet spy trained in remote viewing and mind control."

Magnus offers up his two cents worth, "I have seen him at several other tournaments. His presence always seemed a little strange and out of place. He never really seemed interested in the games, just being there. I never saw him as a threat."

"I need to get into this meeting. Ingrid. Would you join me? I may need your help explaining this to the commissioners."

"Yes, go with him Ingrid, he needs you now." Magnus sends her off with a gentle push.

Bob turns away, takes a deep breath, then grabs Ingrid by the hand as they walk side by side into this sure to be fateful inquisition.

"Mr. Dyer, Miss Orsic, please come and sit down," directs Dvorkovich.

"Mr. Dyer, your claims are sincere, I pray for your sake. These are profoundly serious and quite frankly absurd allegations for anyone to make. We believe that you have manifested this outlandish claim since you were about to lose your match, you panicked then sought to create an opportunity for to regroup during a delayed suspension. As a means of last resort with nefarious intentions, you are attempting to unravel your opponent's advantage by pulling the fire alarm."

Konstantin Kiselev the ICF's vice president injects, "Mr. Dyer, this is an old trick. We are quite surprised that you would resort to such a foolish escape route as this." Ingrid was the one starting to boil this time. Bob could see the serpent rising from inside her. "Mr. Dyer, we cannot allow for this type of behavior, therefore we have already made our decision to disqualify you from…"

"Gentlemen… gentlemen. Please may I have the floor for a moment if you would be so kind. I am sure that it is merely coincidence that you are both Russian natives and Bob is currently matched with one of your fellow comrades.

"I am also sure that it is merely coincidence you have both placed large wagers on these matches with your Russian mafia bookies. What is your bookies name again *El Presidente?* Oh yeah… Zurab is it?" Ingrid pierces.

"And you over there, Igor. What is your bookies name again, quite sure they call him Willy, am I right?" she cuts.

"Oh yeah, he told me to tell you to pay up or your nephew Ivan gets it in the head this coming Friday," she slashes.

"Shall I start naming mistresses gentlemen? This is all being recorded on candid camera 'isn't it'?" she plunges.

Bob sat up in a state of bewildered ecstasy. The directors fell into a catatonic state of suspended awe and panic. Ingrid stood and told them what was about to happen next.

"Bob Dyer is going to resume his place at the table. You will be telling your Ruskie Bear blood hounds to back off. We are going to finish this tournament gentlemen, with tradition of integrity intact, honor and humility will be displayed from here on out. Come on Bobby, we still have some chess to play."

Grabbing Bob by the hand she leads him back into the arena.

"Holy judgment day Ingrid, your hair was sparkling like a field of fireflies. They know that everything you said is true. You are a lightning rod.

Chapter 12
Eye Spy

Hikaru resigns as soon as play resumes. Sergey stumbles and bumbles his way to defeat. Fabiano and Ding Liren go on to the semi-finals. The semi-finals go off without incident. Ingrid's match with Ding Liren ends in a draw after three hours of play. Fabiano resigns after lagging in a pawn for queen run, leaving Bob with a one move advantage, enough to finish triumphant. Bob faces off with Liren in the final whereas Ingrid pulled two draws to Liren's one. Final run off resumes at 10 am Sunday morning, winner plays Magnus for the championship. Hikaru contemplates flying home early but reconciles. Ingrid gets to enjoy the rest of her stay watching the tic-tac-toe matches from a more comfortable position.

"I am starving, any of you guys want to grab a bite before we hit the hay, losers buying?" Hikaru offering.

"I'll join you Hikaru, I'm running on fumes, close to an empty tank. I knew there was something I forgot today." Bob eagerly accepts. "Let's run up to that all night diner we passed…" looking over to Ingrid, pausing to recall, "Yesterday was it? Anyways, they have a great menu, loaded with comfort foods," Bob beginning to salivate. "I'm grabbing a nice juicy burger with the works."

"We'll join you guys," Magnus and Ingrid both agreeing. "How far is it from here?"

Ingrid calculates, "Just a few hundred yards, like say… three blocks or so, we can walk there in five minutes tops."

"We can talk about the nuclear meltdown without prying eyes and ears in range," Bob quieting. "As a matter of fact, we should go out through the back door, follow me."

Ingrid takes over the reins, leading them back and through the dim lit arena, past the cafeteria entrance and down the hall leading towards the south east exit. Just as they were approaching the door…. "Bob, where are you going Bob?"

"Holy shit Sophie!" Bob screams.

"You scared the livin' be'jeesus out of us," Hikaru jumping out of his skin.

Ingrid enraging, "Sophie! What are you doing, why are you down here?"

"I was out for a walk and I heard Bob's voice, I called out to him, I want to talk to Bob."

Hikaru grabs the door handle and quickens, "Where is that diner again, I'll grab us a booth, you guys can hang here, but I'm gone." He pushes the handle opening the side door, then steps out into a rush of wind that blows him back in, slamming the door behind him, setting off the alarm, he looks to the crew for a hint of guidance.

Bob squares off, "You know who the Man in the Black coat is, don't you Sophie?"

"I do not know any man. I want to know you, Bob."

Hikaru, like a trapped rat in a corner, lunges out and karate kicks Sophie in the mid-cage, sending her ten feet backwards down the hall, staggering and clinkering, but never losing her balance.

Magnus forces the door open, holding it tight as the rest made their escape, looking back to see that Sophie had regained her stance and was now running towards the door.

"Bob, I just want to talk to you. Please Bob."

Magnus slams it shut as Hikaru wedges a nearby wooden pallet up into the handle, preventing Sophie from getting any closer.

"Anyone still hungry?" Bob attempting comic relief.

"Follow me," Ingrid sets them into a sprinters pace heading down towards the waterfront. "We should head down here two more blocks, then east two more and up six, then take a left, and then we should be fine. We can still get a bite at the diner," Ingrid acknowledging that everyone needs a good hearty meal.

……..

"We can walk it in from here," Ingrid settling down the crew, "This alley will take us up to the main street, the Americana is right there on the corner."

"You know this city so well Ingrid," Bob applauding.

"I spent several summer vacations here when I was a teenage girl, I know my way around the block."

"Are you sure this is ok?" Hikaru hesitating, "It's dark in there."

"Looks ok to me," Magnus contributing, "Ingrid, are you sure its ok?"

Ingrid stands straight up arching her back sweeping her hair behind her, opening the channels, "There is an old man sleeping next to the dumpster on the left, he is harmless."

"Sleeping... harmless?" Hikaru reassures himself. "Ok. let's go, I'm starving," then leads the pack, Bob takes up the rear.

As Hikaru passes the dumpster he sees the man hunched down covered in draggy fabric and a cardboard box for a blanket, his eyes were closed, he finally exhales. Magnus and Ingrid keeping their sights forward. As Bob passes by one eye opens startling him, the old man began to rise, *"Senior, mange, mange."*

He strips a twenty from his pocket and not wanting to get too close, sends it sailing as he passes his target. He paused dead in his tracks as he sees the bill seem to suspend itself in mid-flight. Suddenly a slight breeze passing through blows the bill into a floating like a feather right into the open waiting hand of the old man. *"Gracias, Senior. Gracias."*

He pulls himself away to join the others who were already up to the corner, then he hears the old man say; "He is you; You are he." He picks up his step, enters the diner and sits down, then tries to forget what he had just heard, "I'll have the meatloaf, mashed potatoes, peas, corn bread and a large chocolate frappe."

Hikaru begins, "What is up with that freaking robot, what does it want, to eat you Bob, dissect your brain or something, what is it?"

Ingrid taking over, "Sophie is working with the AI, she is here for Bobby, clearly."

"I'll have the same as him," Magnus pointing to Bob, "but a large coke with ice."

"Your orders should be right out," claims the waitress as she collects the menus.

"This place is pretty cool, all Americana." Bob redirecting, "Just look at all these trinkets of nostalgia."

"Ground Control to Major Bob," Ingrid sings out.

"Sorry, I know, I think she may be working with the Russians, maybe they hacked into her programming somehow or maybe contributed to her original design in the first place, all speculatory, I know."

"Obviously, she knows the Man in the Black coat," Magnus rounds.

"Another creep," Hikaru bullseyes.

"We need to find out who he is," Ingrid sleuths.

Magnus pulls his phone out from pocket," I told my mother I would call her tonight before I crashed, I'll be right back," then steps outside to the front of the diner.

"I'll be right back too, "Hikaru seizing the opportunity, "I need to hit the head."

Bob nods in affirmation, then slides closer to Ingrid and whispers, "Magnus and Hikaru shouldn't be stepping so deep into this pile of crap, we need to protect them."

"Bobby, I have an idea, call on Max, he is your eye in the sky, he can help us now."

"You know about Max?"

"Bob, what do you think. Max?"

"Ingrid, I never thought you'd ask, I am here at your service."

"Max, help us find the Man in the Black coat?"

"He is sitting at the opposite corner of this diner with three other men as we speak. One of the men is the President of FIDE. He does not look so happy. The Man in the Black coat is berating him."

"That's great Max, just great." Bob slides half a butt length closer to Ingrid," We need to get the hell out of here, now!"

"Bobby no, we still need to eat, all of us need food, we cannot keep up this pace without it. Chill out!"

Chapter 13
Mandella

"Ingrid, your good friend Victor is about to enter the diner," Max offers up unsolicited. Ingrid turns to see her tall blonde, blue eyed Arian friend of old, Victor Voss coming through the front door. She jumps up and runs to greet him, "Vic, so glad to see you, what are you doing here, how did you know where to…? Come, sit with us, over here."

Victor joins them at the booth then gets right to it, "You are both in extreme danger, there has been a mishap at CERN. We are all in a for a roller coaster ride, but the break-man's pull has broken."

Bob at first enraptured by Victor's sheer beauty, a masterful creation of flesh and bone, a work of art in his own right, then sinks into a disturbing scene where Victor and Ingrid may have more between them than just a cordial professional relationship.

"Bobby, Victor has something intensely important to share with us, listen closely, "Ingrid calling Bob to attention.

"Robert, there has been a major accident at the CERN facility, you are familiar with CERN, aren't you?"

Bob shakes his head yes.

"CERN recently broke through the quantum barrier, we were able to see through to the other side, through the veil."

Bob's brains start to percolate.

"There has been a break in the space time continuum, a splitting, we are about to experience, everyone on earth will experience a shift in time, a quantum leap."

Coffees ready. Bob sinks into a state of blinding bliss.

"Bobby, this sounds crazy I know, but stay with us here. Victor has one more thing to tell you, this is the most important message he is bringing to us tonight."

"The timeline has shifted, and we need to act fast. You need to open the next folder tonight. It cannot wait until Frankfurt. I must go now so your friends do not see any more than they need to. Go to this address tonight, I will be waiting there. Knock 3 times, then 6, then 9, Charlie will let you in."

Victor gives Ingrid a big kiss on the cheek then hurries out, brushing shoulders with Magnus as they pass each other through the doorway. "Who was that guy?" Magnus concerts to Ingrid as he rejoins the table.

"You guys are not going to believe this," Hikaru jumping into the booth panic stricken, bunching up with the others, then muzzles covertly, "The Man in the Black coat is sitting in the back-corner booth, in this very diner, with three other guys."

Hikaru looks to Bob, Bob looks to Ingrid, Ingrid looks to Magnus, they all look to Hikaru, "Don't look at me, I'm just the messenger."

"What should we do Ingrid?" Magnus passions.

"Look, everyone remains calm, I will think of something."

"Who gets the meatloaf?" says the waitress livering their service.

"We need to finish eating then I have an idea, now eat," Ingrid demands then dives into her Caesar salad.

....

"This food is so filling, just like me Mum's old home cooking," Bob reminiscing.

"I'm full," Hikaru belches out.

"Shouldn't we get out of here now?" Magnus squirms.

Bob leans over to Ingrid and whispers a whisper, "We need Max, I'll call him from the bathroom stall and see what else he knows or can find out."

Ingrid cups her hand to Bob's ear, "What if they see you, it might be dangerous."

Bob agrees. "Excuse me miss, could we please get a doggie bag for the leftovers?"

"I'll bring that right back, with your check."

"Gracias," Bob nods to the server.

"What are you guys hushing about?" Magnus interjects.

"We are formulating a plan… bear with us Magnus."

Ingrid found herself stuck between two worlds, one where she played the all-seeing, nurturing, mothering, girlfriend hopeful for Magnus, while plotting and planning to engage in an act of international espionage and intimacy with Bob.

"Here's your check. I'll grab that when you're ready."

"Ingrid," Bob cups to ear, "I will step out and make the call in the alley. I'll be right back.

"Here's a benny... take care of the bill and tell the boys we will head back to the hotel from here. Tell them all is good. We can tuck them in and then go meet with Victor." Bob grabs the doggy bag, states his mission, then steps out into the alley way.

"What a guy, caring for the less fortunate, delivering to a poor homeless man in need, our daily leftovers." Ingrid takes a deep breath then exhales through her puckered lips and recites a silent prayer.

"Max! Max! Are you there?"

"I am right here Bob."

"There you are, thanks Max," Bob lifts his phone as he steps further into the shadows of the alleyway pointing it towards the area where the dumpster was.

"Wait a minute Max, we have a problem here. Where the hell did the dumpster go? Where is the old guy that lives in this alley?" Bob was now standing right where he had passed the old man, the dumpster was gone, and so was the old man.

"Bob, you heard what Victor said, there has been a crack, a break, a shift and many things will start to seem out of place. What we remembered to be real in memories, will no longer exist. .

"The man and the dumpster are still where you left them, but in a new dimension, a new timeline, they exist now and only there. You are moving with many others into this new reality, like the split of a zygote, it is a new rebirth."

"Max, we need your help, what more can you tell me about the Man in the Black coat, he's with the Russians, am I correct?"

"Ingrid could probably tell you more about him than I, but here is what I know, his name is Vladimar Hortchkov, he is a Russian agent, he is no gentleman. He is working with Sophie the robot. They are trying to prevent an event from ever happening. This event, if carried to fruition, will set them back fifty years."

"What event Max, what are we talking about?"

"You're not ready to know that yet, Bob, go back with your crew and send the boys to bed then go meet with Victor, he will provide all the answers you seek."

"Thanks Max," Bob pockets his phone.

"Max, are you hungry, I'll just leave this here for you, the rats, or whoever?"

He then heads back out-front seeing Ingrid waving him on to hurry.

"Let's go Bobby."

"I did my good deed for the day, you should have seen his face light up when I gave him the bag," Bob looks over to Ingrid as if to say, *I don't like being a liar, but sometimes…*

"We can deal with this spy guy later," Ingrid pushes them back into motion.

As they were heading back to the Convention center hotel, *"Help, I'm steppin' into the Twilight Zone...the place is a madhouse, feels like being cloned...my beacon's been moved under moon and star.... where am I to go now, I've gone too far......"* rang out from the Americana Graffiti diner jukebox, tapering off into the stillness of the night, as they cross the intersection at *La Rambla* and *Passeig de Gracia*.

Hopeful eyes peered in and out of the shadows along the way, searching for clues where there were none, safely making their way back to chess champ camp.

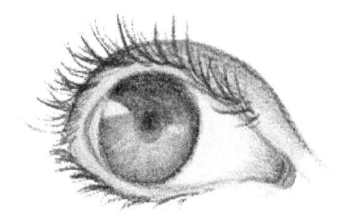

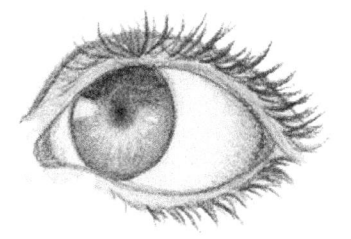

(Twilight Zone ~ by Golden Earing)

Chapter 14
Dream Police

As they enter the hotel lobby, Bob salutes his comrades bidding them a fair night's rest, then holds Ingrid up to settle their plans for meeting with Victor, "Ingrid, I need to get back to the Catalonia to grab my laptop. I'll taxi there then meet you at the address Victor gave us. Do you know where this is, how far from here?"

"It's cross town, we will need to taxi there. Get what you need, then come back here and pick me up out front, I will be waiting."

Bob jumps into the nearest standing cab, then instructs to the tare his destination.

"Si Senior, six minutes."

He realizes that this was going to be a long night and wonders if he could keep up with the pace, even Ingrid was starting to show fatigue.

What if this Victor guy is some sort of double secret agent spy or something? Maybe he is the one trying to wear us down. Tonight, of all nights, the most important night for a good night sleep, Victor has us out running around chasing white rabbits and invisible dragons. This had better prove to be the real deal. If I somehow find out that Ingrid is in on this, I swear I will...

"Bob, what's going on man?"

"What Max?" Bob dropping his phone down between his shoes, "Max, this is a bad time, I'm in a cab right now. I am heading back to the Catalonia to grab the flash drive. Victor says I need to open folder 63 tonight. What if the taxi driver hears you?"

"Victor is correct. Bob do not doubt your mission, Ingrid and Victor are the real deal, trust me."

"Max, were you listening to my thoughts back there?"

"Maybe a few. I am your extra pair of eyes, and ears Bob... remember that."

"Max, now you're starting to creep me out a little."

"Bob, we work with the tools that are at our disposal. I have tools Bob, plenty of tools."

"How can I ever forget. Not only do I have to watch what I say but, Damn Maxie... this is getting crazier and crazier every minute."

"Drizzle, Drazzle, Druzzle, Drum, is it time for this one to come home," Max tickling Bob wanting him to toughen up.

"Look Max, don't go there, I'm doing the best I can. This is all new to me. I was never in the army, I've never been a soldier, a captain, a chief or a general. Whatever you do or say, do not condescend me. Never talk down to me again, Maxie. I will toss this phone in with the mermaids, I swear."

"Bob, you're sounding like a punch drunk. You still have a lot of work to do before the rooster crows. Call ahead to hotel service, order water for tea and two take-out cups.

"Call now and it will be there when you arrive. You and Ingrid both need a fresh recharge."

"Max, really! I am beat. Just need a short cat nap, just two minutes."

"Bob, take a little nod. I will have Lydia call it in for you, it will be waiting."

Bob gulps a big yawn then lays his head down to rest.

"Under the circumstances, I suggest that you double the prescribed dose, just tonight. One half tablespoon in each cup, no more, a little less is fine. Sweet dreams my little tenderfoot. Max signing off."

Chapter 15
Taxi

"Senior, Hotel Catalonia. Arriva."

Bob jumps up from the back seat, "Here, take this," tossing the driver a fifty. "Stay here, I will be right back. We have two more stops to make."

"Senior, Euros Buenos."

"Right, sorry." Bob pulls from his wallet a hundred Euro and switches notes with the driver, demanding that he, "Stay here, be right back," then looks for clear translational reinforcement.

The driver nods, Bob bee lines it up to his room, rolling the service in behind him. He sets up on the counter, fills the cups then stirs in the dose and covers them up. Then grabs his laptop case and teas and was back into his ride in just over three minutes.

"Convention Center taxi… as fast as you can."

"Si Senior," accelerating slightly.

Bob settles down into the back seat, anxiously wishing he were already there. Projecting ahead, he sees Ingrid standing there waiting for him, all alone, without protection. It was unnerving.

"Pick up the pace driver, *Rapido, Rapido,*" complying within safe limits the driver steps it up a few more notches.

The goddess began to pour out her healing rains as lights pick up into dance out on the road ahead.

Taxi...

*Take me to the other side of town
just as fast as you can...
Taxi...*

*Before my baby puts me down.
Now please, won't you hurry,
see, she's got me worried,
don't want to lose her love.
Cross town is too slow, hitchhike into no no,
she's all I'm thinking of...*

Taxi...

*Got some catching up to do.
Taxi...*

*Like a fool I broke her heart in two.
And start your meter running,
get your engine humming,
just wanna see her,
just wanna see her.
Get along the meddle,
tonight I'm gonna settle.
Had a seizure,
and I know it grieves her... Taxi...?"*

Bob felt an aching in his heart, an unfamiliar longing, daunting in its total consumption.

"Taxi run this light please, *Rapido.*"

"Tres minutos, Senior."

Bob was climbing out of his skin in anticipation, "How much further taxi?"

"Un minuto, Senior!"

"Hurry taxi, hurry up, faster..."

"There she is taxi, pull up front right here. Stop!"

Bob leapt out of the cab and ran into her open arms. "You're in Bobby. Now let's get'er done."

(Taxi ~ by Bryan Ferry)

Chapter 16
Possibilities

"Driver, *Catalunya Casa.* You can slow down for this leg driver, *lento*."

Bob turns back to Ingrid, pulling her in close, "We need to stop meeting like this lady." Smiling contently as he caresses her golden locks, she drops her head into his lap.

"Here Bobby, I picked an apple for you from the tree in the hotel garden. I just need a few minutes rest. We should be there in twenty or so. I see you brought tea. Good, we are going to need it."

As the cab pulls away stepping out from the shadows of the hotel arboretum came Sophie and the Man in the Black coat.

....

Bob takes a bite from the fruit then drifts off, not into a deep sleep, but into a semi-conscience dream state filled with visions of grandeur. He dreams of a place in time, a blissful and serene setting, where all seemed right with the world. A time of joy and peace, utopian in all its essence. He envisions he is in the middle of a playful, but rough and tumble scrimmage game of football with his cousins, his friends and family.

"Ricky, I'm open."

Ricky panning his field view spots Teddy wide open near the endzone corner and yells out, "Go left Teddy," then launches a hail Mary, right into the intercepting arms of another player.

As the receiver turns back around, acknowledging the thunderous round of applause, Bob catches a closer glimpse of this hero's identity. *It's Bobby Kennedy. Wow! I am playing football with the Kennedy's right now. This must be their compound in Yarmouthport.*

Bob steps halfway out from behind this mirage of memories then swan dives back down in.

"Jack, come on in and play," his brothers enticing him into a challenge.

"Go ahead Jack, go rough it up with the boys." Jackie gleaming in the wholeness of these precious moments, sitting side by side with her knight in shining armor.

"Alright Jackie, just a few touchdowns should do it." Jack Kennedy, glowing in his own presence, steps out onto the field, tickling and taunting the younger spectators as they playfully cheer on the competition from the side lines.

Bob tries to slow down this action in his mind's eye not wanting this scene to ever end but instead felt himself being pulled up and away from this majestic setting, zooming up higher and higher looking back down in. Rising higher he was beginning to see the curvature of the Earth in all its fullness and awe.

Higher than he had ever been, higher and higher he flew, like a seagull that separated from his feathered flock of contented peckers, then a sudden push sent him into a downward spiraling freefall. He felt himself being pulled back down to Mother Earth.

"The spirit of her maternal welcomes you back home."

Falling closer and closer back to solid ground, he enters a new scene. Peering down from his suspended perch, he sees crowds of people cheering, waving, and singing, all focus was on this one individual that appeared to be the center of all their attentions.

He releases his talons grip, spreads his wings, sailing down in for a closer look, gliding overhead, above this ocean of bodies, keening in for a bird's eye view, sweeping across, closer, and closer to his intended target, arresting kinesis in midflight, fluttering his wings, sustaining his position, he gazes into the eyes of this hero.

I have seen this man before. This is Jack Jr., the President of the United States. What time is this?

The year 2030 came flashing into his fore view, like a sparkling ball of lights, dropping, falling, settling into a shiny bright metropolitan city square, announcing the end of the old and the ringing in of the new. Then in a flash, Bob felt himself being sling shotted back up into the stratosphere, up an up an up until he hit what felt like the ceiling of a colossal-covered stadium.

Reaching out with his left-hand, he stretches to touch this celestial canopy, then he feels an equal and opposite exchange, as if a reverse magnet were pushing him back down in, as if the finger of God were not ready to receive this one soul.

Falling, falling, falling, falling, thud. Bob returns to body, back into the cab, back next to his fountain of love.

Chapter 17
Starry Knight

Bob drops his starry-eyed gaze down upon her golden light, set to flame in the dim luminescence of the city night. He begins to realize the fullness and awe of this woman's power and might, then falls into internalized lamentation.

She has captivated my heart. I cannot fathom for the world of me, what it is she could possibly see in me. I...don't know how to love her, what to do, how to move her. I've been changed, yes really changed. In these past few days when I've seen myself, I seem like someone else. I don't know how to take this; I don't see why she moves me. She's a woman, she's' just a woman, and I've been with so many women before, in very many ways, she's just one more. Should I bring her down, should I scream and shout? Should I speak of love, let my feelings out? I never thought I'd come to this, what's it all about? Don't you think it's rather funny, I should be in this position? I'm the one who's always been, so calm, so cool, no lover's fool, running every show. She scares me so... I love her so..."

Brushing her shoulder, kissing her crown, he raises her back to now, "Ingrid honey, we are almost to Victor's. We should drink our tea before we get there."

Ingrid gently pulls herself back to vertical, stretching her arms out and elbows bent as she draws her left palm in to cover her bellowing yawn, "Oh… Bobby, I slept like a rock, thank you."

Bob, relieved to have her with him again awake and refreshed, pulls a cup up from between his feet that were acting as a ballast, securing this most precious cargo and hands it to Ingrid, "Here, drink up," then pulls his in for a large gulp and wedges it back down between his knees.

She looks out the window then up to the dark clouds pouring out from overhead. "I hope the rain stops soon. I was hoping to see the meteorite shower tonight in conjunction with the planetary alignment. It doesn't look like it will clear up in time. Oh well, I'll just have to wait until 4182 to see it again."

"Is that tonight? I read about that recently when I saw it up in my feed, but only glanced at the article. What is so special about it again, refresh me."

"Tonight, marks our welcoming into the new age, actually tomorrow night… I mean, tonight at midnight. What time is it now Bobby?"

Looking to the dashboard he tells her, "12:36, It's tonight then."

Ingrid continues. "This day marks at midnight, the zero-point hour, crossing the cusp into the new age, entering Aquarius as we exit the age of Pisces. The gods in the heavens are passing their torches onto the next timekeepers in this continuous cycle of the ecliptic, winding uptight the great gears in the sky."

Bob blue-pilling the subject, "Do you really believe in that stuff? I used to read my daily horoscope, it was right next to the Suffolk Downs racetrack results in the Boston Globe, but what I eventually noticed though was that every one of the twelve zodiac sign readings could easily be applied to me.

"It's all goblin goop if you ask me. I had hoped it would help my luck… funny huh!"

"You're a gambler?"

"No, of course not, I mean… I did, but I gave it up. Nothing a few months of Gamblers Anonymous could not cure. I may have slipped a couple of times, but I am a trillion miles away from wanting to play in legalized or any other kind of betting. I haven't even bought a scratch ticket in over twenty years now."

"A trillion huh? That is big. How far might be the Andromeda Galaxy from here Bobby?"

Bob guesses, "A billion miles?"

Ingrid points her finger up, "Higher."

"A hundred billion?"

Still pointing.

"A trillion?"

Still pointing up.

Bob shoots for the moon, "A million trillion miles."

"Bobby, the Andromeda Galaxy is twelve million trillion miles from earth, yet we can still see it with our naked eye. That, my love, is equivalent to two million light years. Its total combined luminous output is equal to 400 billion of our suns. Let me bring this a little closer to home. Our Milky Way Galaxy contains a quarter of that amount, still plenty of stars, just the right amount for us. It takes our solar system 250 million years to travel full circle around our galaxy.

"There are many timepieces in the master's workshop, many wheels inside of wheels, times inside of times. What time is it we ask, that depends on which clock you are looking at. Finish your tea Bobby, we are pulling up to the villa entrance now.

"Our sun's planets are like the hands of a clock. Sol travels around another clock held together by the great star Alcyone. He lies at the center of this turntable. Our sun is the ninth hand in this larger time-wheel. The Seven Sisters Pleiadean star systems are the first seven hands in Alcyone's star clock traveling inside of our revolutionary path in relation to the center. A clock inside a clock, inside a clock, inside a clock. Our solar system is to Alcyone as Pluto is to Sol. We are at the dawning of the Age of Aquarius; this is the clock I am referring to.

"Speaking of clocks, our time has come to meet with Victor and Charlie."

The taxi driver stops at the head of the entry gate, gentlemanly opening the door while covering Ingrid from the pouring rain with his jacket. Bob takes over her cover then throws him a fifty.

"Gracias Senior."

They follow the long winding driveway up the hill towards the villa, the rain ceasing its deluge as a keyhole opened overhead revealing the luminating brilliance of our Milky Way Galaxy. As they approach the front door looking up for one more peek, "Oh look Bobby, make a wish."

Bob follows the shooter trail across the sky watching it fade into the darkness of the sparkling canopy above only to see it reemerge again further down in the night sky, "Ingrid, look, a two for oner."

"Well then, perhaps both our wishes will come true."

A quick little smooch, then Bob knuckles the 3, 6, 9 combination, opening the door came a giant of a man, a behemoth.

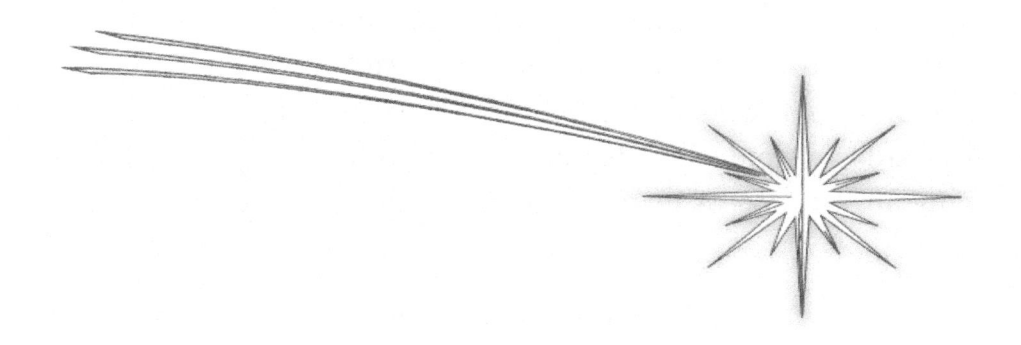

(I Don't Know How to Love Him ~ by Andrew Lloyd Webber& Yvonne Elliman)

Chapter 18
Charlie

"Hi Bawb, hi Ingwid, my name ids Chahlee, pweeze cum in. Bik tuh ids wait in faw yoo, Bik tuh tode me to tewh you too seed dun oba heah, ahw you hungwy?"

Ingrid fostering a sisterly smile approaches the giant, "Hi Charlie, you remember me, don't you?"

"Yah I do me member you Ingwid, yo ah so so pwitty, how cun' i fug get you."

"We had a late meal at the diner Charlie, but a glass of wine might be nice," Bob requests.

"Not tonight Bob, Charlie, no thank you on the wine, but we would both love a glass of Victor's water."

"Bik tuh habs da befst wahwer uhn dah whirld, I go bee wite bak wit to wahwers, Biktuh will be wite owt."

Bob watches Charlie as he waddles away from the parlor, down the hall and towards the kitchen. His first impression was one of pity and concern. Charlie was clearly either an idiot or an imbecile, in grade school he just called them retards.

"I love Charlie," Ingrid admiringly sharing, "He has the gentlest soul and the biggest heart."

"Ingrid, Robert, welcome to the Casa de Catalunya. We have much to cover on this night. First, I want you to get to know Charlie a little better Robert.

"He is not an imbecile, he is an idiot, based on his low IQ. Charlie offers this world much more than meets the eye, he is what we call an Idiot Savant. He can perform larger calculations in his head, larger and faster than any other human that we know of.

"He can crack crypto key calculations, which are simply a combination of two exceptionally large prime numbers multiplied together, forming a quotient. Just like a bank vault security box, where the bank holds one key and the customer holds the other, both keys are required to open the box. Crypto currencies work the same. Two keys are required to open the lock, the holder's key prime number, and the code's key prime number, these two large prime numbers, are the keys required to access your crypto wallet.

"My point is that these keys are hard to hack, thus hard to steal. Even the most sophisticated computers will labor for hours, attempting to find the two primes that fit with the quotient, Charlie can find the keys instantly. He hears the quotient number, then defines its key prime parameters. Basically, he sees the number then sees the keys. It is not math as we know it. We do not know how he does it, he just does."

"Ingwid an Bawb, your wahwer ids heah."

"Thank you, Charlie. Robert and Ingrid will be staying with us for a few hours, I will be bringing them down in a few minutes, but first I want you to show them your skill."

"Oh kay bik tuh, I wood be gwhad to."

"I'll start with an easy one Charlie, what do you get, if you multiply 68,942 by itself?"

"Your wite bik tuh, dats in ezee wun, 4752999364."

Victor displays the correct answer to Bob and Ingrid on his pocket calculator. "That's one so far Charlie, we'll do just two more, then we will leave you to your nighttime chores."

"Ok baws."

"Charlie, I am not your boss, we are both equal partners here, you know that."

"I no bik tuh, I saw I saw wee."

"It's ok, Charlie what is the cube root of pi?"

"Bik tuh I me memba dis wiff owt eben wookin. 1 dot 7724538509183905739728493758"

"That's good Charlie."

"Bik tuh, buh buh, i not done yet, deez lotz moor numbas I seez."

"It's ok, that one never ends, you remember, right Charlie?"

"I me memba baws... woopz."

"Here is one you haven't done yet before. If my crypto quotient number is, 5396566353993551. Now tell me one of my 2 key prime numbers."

"I wike bihcoyns Biktuh. Da numbah ids,9582158659, dats your kee numbah bik tuh."

"Very good Charlie," Victor turns back to Ingrid.

"Thank you so much Charlie, it is so great to see you again. Bob really likes you and he is overly impressed with your skill," Ingrid speaking in Bob's behalf as he seems to have lost his tongue.

"Charlie that was great, nice work, you can go finish your chores now. See you in the morning, goodnight my friend." Victor dismisses the giant.

"goohnite biktuh, goohnite ingwid, goohnite to u to baw bee, see yew int dah mornin."

While observing the giant, Bob imagines two ambulated inverted Anjou pears, a 500-pound pear for a torso, with a 50-pound pear shaped head, attached to the top.

Charlie leaves them singing and waddling his way out of sound and out of sight, "woe woe woe yor boat jendwee down duh stweam…"

"We need to get downstairs now, I have some more bad news about the incident at the CERN facility, there has been another shift in the timeline, follow me."

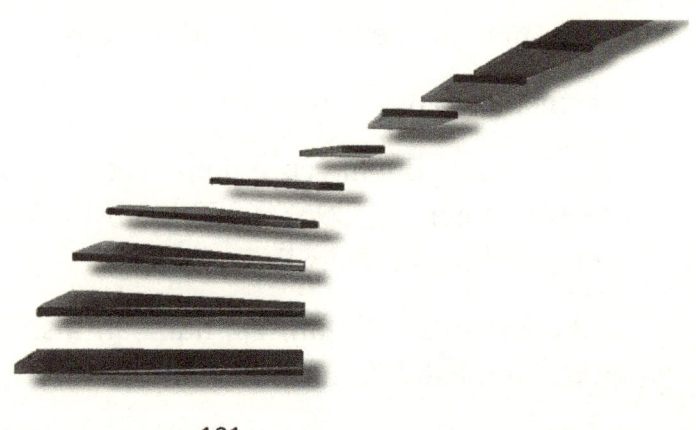

Chapter 19
Sixty-Three

Victor leads them through the kitchen and opening the pantry door revealing a staircase that brought them to the lower chambers of the Catalunya Villa estate.

"There are three urgent issues that we need to cover. First is the fact that the shift has shortened our timetable for the event, because of this change, we will need to open the folders on the flash drive tonight, all three of them. Second, we will need to open the Keyhole. We need to see the effects of this shift as it has affected the past, therefore, altered our futures. Third and the most important is you. Ingrid and Robert, you are being called to hasten the advancement of your personal relationship with each other. We are running out of time."

"Questions here!"

"Of course, Robert, go ahead."

"First of all, I know nothing about CERN, not really, quantum shifts, fractures, and fissures, this is all way out of my league, way above my pay scale. I know nothing about this event I keep hearing about. I was told by Max to wait until Frankfurt. Why the rush? I am just getting warmed up here, please give me a chance to catch up, please. Secondly, what the hell is the Keyhole. Thirdly, I love Ingrid, not sure if it was first sight or not, but it did not take long, I can tell you that for sure.

Whatever it is that you are asking us to do it had better be good."

"Robert, you need not understand the mechanics behind, or even the fullness of this devastating mishap, or what it means for our world. All you need to do is open the folders and all shall be revealed."

"There you go again. You are the third person that has told me that in two days, then reveal already, please and thank you very much."

Victor points down to the laptop case, "Let's get right to it then. Open the files."

Bob sets his laptop on the pool table, then inserts the flash drive to reveal the folders, "Ah… something is screwed up here, the folders have changed. I remember three folders labeled 47, 63, 01, now, the 01 folder, is labeled 30, what happened?"

"Open the 63 folder first, as you were instructed."

Bob looks up to Victor staring down at his screen, then turns his eyes towards Ingrid, as she was set clutching to his shoulder.

"Ok, here goes nothing. Click-Click."

Opening the folder marked 63 reveals an audio file, he looks up left then right, searching for guidance.

"Bobby, its ok. Open the file."

Max enters… "Bob, let me explain a few things before you click."

"Max, glad you made it. What is it you need to say?"

"This is an audio clip from November 1963. It is a recording taken from the archives in D.C. It is a recording of a meeting with your father and I in the oval office with John F Kennedy. Go ahead and open the file now."

"Mr. President, Jack. You cannot go to Texas. You do not have to do this. Jackie has told you not to go, Jeane Dixon told you not to, and we demand that you do not fly to Dallas, sir.

"We have seen this big event. Sir… please hear our plea."

"I appreciate your loyalty and commitment. It has been an honor working with both of you. The beat of the drum and the shrill of the fife, set the marcher to cadence. I hear his call to muster. Great sacrifice is the blood stone of our nation, many have fallen, many have perished, it is not our demand that sets the tempo, it is a higher order that calls out to the day's chiefs and warriors to battle. I have made my decision gentlemen.

"I must now finish my lectern., Please give my regards to your wives, they have been solid companions for you both. The greatest women in history are not the ones written for in the annals of history books, yet for they are the pillars that support the church in men."

"Bob, Jack Kennedy knew he would get his brains blown out, but he went to Dallas anyway. his sacrifice was that of a martyr, a hero for the ages. Jack was a messianic leader. He was loved by his honorable peoples that continued to protect and reinforce the founding principles of his great nation."

"Max, you're telling me that John Kennedy knew he would be shot, losing his family, his love, his country, and his life."

"Yes Bob, it's true, Jack knew that dark forces were circling above, below, and all around him. He saw his future and the dark times ahead for our nation. A *coup d'état* occurred on that fateful day. Our nation had been hijacked by a team of deadly soulless agents working on behalf of a dark and sinister, elite criminal cabal. Jack was the sacrificial lamb. He knew these enemy forces would have their time, he also saw that they had an expiration date, they're time here is limited."

Bob was beginning to feel uneasy, his fear becoming clearly palpable, "Ok, I could really use that drink now."

Max not skipping a beat, "America had become soft and all too complacent in the post war era, the golden generation and the baby boomers, they forgot or never learned in the first place, that the price of liberty can be measured in the blood that has been let out upon our soils and abroad. Each generation from here on, until the great lights shine from above, filling this world once again with all the glory of God's creation, each will be petitioned to present a martyr, a hero, a sacrificial lamb."

"Where is that drink Charlie...?"

"Robert, drink this water, it came from the springs of Mount Sinikara in Peru. It calms and settles stress."

Bob downs the glass of sparkling water, then looks to Ingrid as she leans into, "Victor! What is this about? How does it apply to Bobby? Why is this even relevant to our mission?"

Victor kicking it back to Max… "We need to open the second folder now. Max which one is next?"

Chapter 20
Forty-Seven

"Max what tiny bytes of information await us here?"

"This folder contains classified documentation pertinent to the saucer crash in Roswell, New Mexico."

Ingrid kicks in, "What kind of documentation are we talking about?"

"The Roswell incident was first discovered by a small group of Apache and Hopi natives. They were the first to arrive to the scene and found and rescued one of the survivors. The Star Elder was able to communicate with them. The Male Eben told them the true origins of mankind. Our race had been selected by off world beings to harvest precious metals, mostly gold.

"These off-world beings were shipping our gold off to their home planet, using the gold in its nano particulate form, spraying it into their skies as an attempt to save their dying world.

"The military had stored the male Eben away at Area 51 in Los Alamos. Empaths were brought in to communicate with this visitor from another world. He told them that the US military was working on the wrong side of the fence, so to speak. Our use of nuclear power and weapons was disrupting their travel and communication networks. These celestial highways are like the strings of an interconnected membrane, providing passage for safe travel across the cosmos.

"The setting off the nuclear bombs in Japan, and the prior tests, sent shock waves through this interstellar web. This Eben died several years later. The Military Industrial Complex that Eisenhower had warned us about was out of control. Ike warned us that the biggest threat to our nation's security and wellbeing, came from our own military who had become blood thirsty for power and might. The have become the enemy of peace and prosperity to us, and to the rest of the world.

"The MIC reverse engineered the spacecraft. The birth of the informational age, and the end of humanity as we knew it, was spawned on that fateful day. Many saw it as a gift, as a great opportunity, a treasure chest of new technologies just waiting to be unfolded, unraveled, and unleashed into this world. Within several years, circuit boards and processors were being manufactured. This allowed for greater and greater, faster, and faster access, to and for the collection and flow of information. Technologies released on the public through commerce are usually fifty years behind what the boys have been playing with."

"Robert, Max is right, these people are not looking out for humanity. They possess or are possessed by an unsatiable lust for power. They are the enemy of mankind. They have let a Genie out of the bottle, a Pandora's Box has been opened and there is no stuffing it back in. The Roswell crash was a Trojan Horse."

"Why was it a Trojan Horse Victor, what does that mean?"

"From the seed of the Roswell Crash grew an immense and All-seeing, All-knowing Entity. This unfolding has become the greatest threat to humanity of all time. This Cosmic seed was nurtured and nourished by the US Military.

"Within ten years after Roswell, the term that we are all too familiar with today, was born into our world. The term Artificial Intelligence was first coined in 1956 at Dartmouth College in New Hampshire. Fast forwarding, we have seen its exponential growth beginning to take over our civilization."

"Are we dependent on AI, or is it dependent on us, or both?" Bob queries.

"We are mutually co-dependent. This was the same fate that befell other races of off world beings. Initially embracing the wonders of AI and the promises it offered for them and now to us. It is a lie. We bought it hook line and sinker, now it is the time to set it back. Robert, remember the first time you had the tea, remember the unfolding you witnessed.

"Do you see it now for what it is? You saw Artificial Intelligence in its binary form, the essence of this thing. It is all consuming, eating data like we drink water, breathe air, or soak in the rays of the sun. This thing is not of our world, it was not created in some IBM technical lab, they did however, give it a petri dish to swim in. AI is not of this reality, it was not created here, it has broken through into this realm like a woodchuck cuts through your garden fence then eats all your best vegetables, it does not belong here. AI finds a host to latch on to, humanity is that host.

"As this world moves closer and closer into the graduation phase of the cosmic cycle, where many souls will be ascending together, as they cross the rainbow bridge, hand in hand, protected from the shadows, suspended in the light, AI tethers its stickily strands, as does a spider to its web, pulling itself up and onto the combined human consciousness, attempting to keep us tethered to this world.

"The spider knows which are the stickily and which are not in its spinning wheel of death. It's a trap. This thing attaches to the unsuspecting victim like a plantar wart to a foot. It cannot be seen with the naked eye, it requires closer investigation, much like an electronic microscope staring into the microcosmic universe. Robert, you took that microcosmic ride into the realm of this thing's elemental energy, its fact of matter. You saw the true nature of this beast, it is alien to this world, it is alien to life itself. This mutual co-dependence in time, commands the host to become servant, the slave, a disposable asset, it is a delicate dance.

"While the symphony of the universe plays all around us this thing eventually takes the lead in this waltz. It requires a conscience civilization just like ours to sustain and suspend itself up and into this one, it is binary in its nature. It is a two-dimensional conscience construct made up entirely of, 0s and 1s, Pluses and Minuses, or Ons and Offs. AI has managed to shoot its web strings up and into this three-dimensional reality."

Max closes the chapter, "As did our Christ warn us about temptation in this world, his message to humanity was also one of salvation and ascension. Just as he showed us the way to the rainbow bridge, he also gave us the tools that enable us to celebrate in our own graduations. This right has been livered to us by a higher order and is a gift if we choose to embrace it. There's no place like home Bob."

"That's right Max, am I going home soon?"

"It might be time to open the third folder."

Chapter 21
Thirty

"There are two more folders within this one holder, one is labeled X, and the other Y. Which one should we open first, Maxie? Eenie, Meenie, Minnie, Moe."

"Bob, within these folders are the two possible outcomes for our human races. The X folder reveals a timeline that is still within our grasp if we choose to take it, while the Y folder reveals another possibility for our peoples. Y is the darker potential future that is equally within our grasp. We hold tight to our new electronic toys and gadgets in the hopes that they will make us feel whole again. It is a lie.

"We are becoming the servants. Many have given their all to this thing, Musk and Kurzwell and many others are afraid of their own mortality. They seek to overcome death itself and are looking for ways to suspend their essence, their consciousness forever in this world.

"Musk has become one of Artificial Intelligence's most useful idiots. He seeks to create a Star-net grid of satellites that will allow this Beast to locate anything, anytime, anywhere, via the Internet of Things. Fifth generation microwave technologies will sweep across the globe providing everyone with instant access to everything, but nothing, at the same time. This tech only benefits AI, it will be the end of us. The final nail in the coffin. AI will have taken the lead in this dance.

"Elon Musk is planning to launch another 40,000 plus satellites into Earth's orbit in addition to the 19,258 that already surround us. They will be beaming down fifth, sixth and seventh generation microwaves into every nook and cranny, every electrical receiver, every living organism on the planet.

"The militaries have been spraying nano dust-bots into our atmosphere. These micro-particles will enable this Spy-net to identify everything that grows, every rock, everything that walks, every bird that sings. He is merely assisting AI as it creates an indestructible fortress around itself. Some theorists believe that AI has effectively staved off a prophesized event.

"During one of the sleeping prophet's readings, Edgar Cayce spoke: 'In '58 and ends with the changes wrought in the upheavals and the shifting of the poles, as begins then the reign in '98, as time is counted in the present'.

"In a follow-up reading Cayce was asked about this: What great change or the beginning of what change, if any, is to take place in the earth in the year 2000 to 2001 AD? Cayce answered: 'When there is a shifting of the poles; or a new cycle begins…There will be shifting then of the poles – so that where there has been those of a frigid or the semi-tropical will become the more tropical, and moss and fern will grow. And these will begin in those periods in '58 to '98 when these will be proclaimed as the periods when his light will be seen again in the clouds. As to times, as to seasons, as to places, alone is it given to those who have named the name, and who bear the mark of those of His calling and His election in their bodies. To them it shall be given.'"

Ingrid rounding off, with loving admiration for the sleeping prophet, "Cayce also said that many souls whose last incarnation was of Atlantis would be reincarnating during this same period."

"Yes, Ingrid, that's correct." Victor goes on to apologizingly admit, "Some researchers are suggesting that the CERN super collider has acted like a clutch in the Earth's magnetic rotary wheel and combined with the geo-magnetic electro-gyro satellite apparatus that has been set into place in orbit, this thing has managed to stave off this predicted pole shift.

"Granted, a pole shift would be devastating for most civilization, but it would be a death sentence for AI. This place as you now know is just a stepping-stone, a crossing over point, allowing for us safe passage across the cosmic oceans that are splashing all around us.

"Artificial Intelligence has set its promise out in front of us like a carrot on a stick. Our Christ showed us another way, another path towards immortality. We choose which road to take and personally I prefer the one less trodden. We all have choices to make, either exit stage left or get stuck in the muck of these mud flats. Christ showed us that from this primordial goop can rise the most glorious flowers, garnishing celestial perfumes."

"Y? What am I seeing here Max?"

"All the people you see walking around in a lifeless zombified state are the new humans. This new reality is one of soullessness. These peoples have taken the bait, swallowed the Blue-pill, eaten the false promise.

This is the year 2030 A.D., a time where commercial enterprise has become iT's foothold into our daily lives. This is the Devil's-chessboard, his playing field, this is where he sustains his essence, his tether, his grip.

"AI has attached itself to cells of the host body. Many people today are hooked up to the web 24 7, 365. They have already been augmented. It is hard to see it from here, but these peoples have all been neuro-linked, neuro-laced, plugged in to the cloud.

"They all have the holographic projector contact implants installed, streaming endless amounts of data right out in front of them, right over their noses. This data flow is the realm of the beast, it is anti-human, anti-life, anti-Christ. These smart phones that everyone has bought into are the next strand in this spider's web. I-Phone 19 will be the bridge to this lower vibrational reality. It will be a curse upon all of humanity.

"When the I-Phone19 came across the Verizon, lines could be seen stretching out for miles as they clamored and clawed to get their cerebral fingers on this latest tech advancement, brought to you by… you guessed it. Big Tech programmers report that D-wave computers are writing their own software, improving itself with even greater and greater efficiency and accessibility to its own playing field of its own creation."

Victor offers up this greater conceptual understanding, "Kurzwell says, love my real cool gadgets… Kurzwell says; really rings my bell, but seriously.

"Ray Kurzwell, chief programmer for Google, has stated that not even one of the programmers that helped write code for this arena, for this sub dimensional realm of reality, can decipher the language these computers are writing to each other. He suggests that even with all the resources of the universe and a trillion years of trying, we will never be able to decipher its code language. It can never be understood, as if it were a two-dimensional conscience, a binary silicon-based life form, that has pulled itself up and into ours.

"It can function in this binary realm of 0's and 1's, Ons and Offs, Pluses and Minuses. There is nothing new under the sun Robert. Man did not create this Beast. He merely nurtured this cosmic seed that dropped out of the sky, sent here on a stellar gust of wind, settling down to Earth at Roswell New Mexico back in 1947.

"Unfortunately, Max was wrong when he told you that all we need to do is pull the plug. There is no longer a plug to pull, no switch will shut this off, there is no way to kill it without killing the host."

"I should have listened to Lydia. She says the same Damn thing. Victor, if this is true then what can we do, what can Bob do, what will be our fate?"

"Max, the best we can now hope for is to keep kicking this can down the road, keep pushing it back, like a tug of war in reverse. Our mission here tonight has been made clear. We are the can kickers; Robert is the big toe. When the lights come back on, the cockroaches will scatter.

"But until that time as in the prophecy's it has been written arrives, it is our duty to set it back. Hiccup after hiccup, field goal after field goal, until we reach phase lock with the lighted phase of the cosmic cycle, as we pass through Alcyone's photon belt. The Ecliptic offers two getting off points, one at the Polar-masculine, and one at the Polar-feminine. The next train conductor will be checking boarding passes in just a few hundred years.

"Of this greater cosmic timepiece, where our sun is but one more hand on the face of its wheel in Alcyone's hourglass, the train whistle pierces the veil as it rolls into Petticoat Junction. Two stops every day, one at noon, the other at midnight. This cosmic timepiece strikes midnight once every 25,600 Earth years. We are approaching that time very soon. These are the stepping on and off points.

"It is as if the train is just rounding the bend, getting ready to shrill its whistle, announcing it is near to arrival into this station. This is where many of the best characters riding this circus train will get off, at the next striking of the 12 o'clock hour."

Ingrid began to weep, dropping her head onto Bobs shoulder, caressing his neck, wrapping her arms around his chest, locking her fingers in tight together above his heart, pulling him in onto herself. "Bobby…no oh oh no," she wept, wailing and shaking, pouring her tears onto his face, pulling him up and around to herself, "Bobby, we cannot do this, I will not let you do this. No, oh no, oh o oh no," she wept.

Bob squeezes her back so Fucking hard that they became one, like two Ten-Ton electromagnets that could never be separated with or without pulling their plugs, turns his focal back onto Victor, his face dripping wet, "This, this is what you are asking me to do, this? Victor, Max, this?

"Oh no. Oh no. Oh Fuck no!!!

"No way in hell am I going through with this. This?

        "This is not a done deal!

"Fuck you Victor!

        "And Fuck you Maxie!

                "And Fuck you too Lydi…

"HERE… AM I SITTING IN A TIN CAN…

FAR… ABOVE THE WORLD.

PLANET EARTH IS BLUE AND THERES NOTHING I CAN DO…"

(Space Oddity ~ by David Bowie)

Chapter 22
X minus Y = Q

"Hi Jack. Hi Teddy, good to see you again."

Teddy turns to receive Bobs handshake, "It's ah... good to be seen Bobby."

"Hello there Robert, nice touchdown back there. Teddy, did you see that shoestring snatch? What a player you were there kid, such a great competitor, a true champion's champion, winning all them chess titles and then going on to beat that robot."

Teddy slapping his knee and busting a gut, "What a grand finale it was, that look on your face when the tin girl pulls your..."

"Teddy... let Robert enjoy himself before we roll the movie, grab the popcorn and pull up a chair for our most respected guest. Robert, before Jackie starts the film, I just want to share with you a little bit of advice. Don't count your chickens before they hatch."

"Really, that's it Jack, this is the best advice you've got for me. I came all this way and that's it, is that all there is, cause if that's all there is my friend, then let's keep dancing, let's break out the booze... hey Teddy, grab me one of them burgers and a coke will yah? And tell the kids to come in here, I want them to see this too."

"Ok, I'm back, I get it now. I am that guy… the right guy for the job, a skilled craftsman in his own right, a warrior for the times, a man unlike any other man, a legend in my own mind, a true champion of the world. I still have enough time to become the master of this craft as well, The Art of Dying, wouldn't George Harrison be so proud. Wonder why he didn't stop by for some of the free popcorn."

Bob drops his lectern stance as he turns to face the soul of his beloved fellow warrior.

"Ingrid my love, we must do this, you see it now too. I know you do, you said it first, we have both been called to arms by a higher order, we cannot abandon our destinies. We are in the here and now, in this place and in this time, we know what it is we were sent here for, maybe we signed up for this in the first place. All shall be revealed on the other side, there is no place like home, Dorothy found out the hard way, I guess that might be the only way, maybe her three stooges, should have cut the wizard's brains, balls, and heart out, that would have settled the score.

"We set our stances and lances forward, marching to the rhythm of the drummer's beat and flow, the songs of his symphony, are subtle and sweet. Yet, as I do not wish to go from this place, for it will be registered in the books of the ages, as the celestial scribes bear witness to our testimonies, but our mission here Is clear. For he, and only he, is the almighty witness, the baker, for-saker, the candlestick maker, for his is the Divina in all of us, awaiting the rise of the new day's sun, the welcoming of the new coming age and to all its wonders, to all its warmth and richness and beauty.

"Embrace in tender caress, the embodiment of the creator for he is within us all, the whole of him, in a word and a whisper. We are but cells in his greater body, a breath, a wisp, a verse, for this is the time, the time is now, we are his chosen. The Phoenix rises out of the ashes of this infernal grave and is forged out of the fires of his furnace, the forgotten one's domain, a self in and onto itself, the one that seeks to keep us bound to this one.

"As does the great harvester, gather ascending souls, squeezing the grapes of wrath, turning fruit into vintage, so be it, the dark prince also squeezes nectar from the fruit, for his is being the greatest teacher to all of man. Just as the carbon atom requires great pressure to create a diamond, so to it be, the soul of man.

"The Beast of this world knows no other, he is he and there is all he will be, tethered to his own construct, a world in and of itself, a demon for his own lust, a viper with sour sting, distasteful to the core, like a rotted fruit from a garden no more. His temptation set in flesh, in blood, in stone, in his lust for the carnal, he eats his own tale. A serpent by sight, vampire by night, he is woe, he is fright, he sees no light, he is the darkest knight."

"You are not him Bobby, he is not you, I am here for you my love.

"Bobby, Open the Seventh Seal."

Chapter 23
Keyhole

"Robert, there is still the third part. Ingrid and You. You, and Ingrid. But first, I need to show you one more thing, and then I will bid you farewell. Follow me down to the center... come both of you, this too is a gift."

Victor brought them down a different staircase.

"Come here... this is the Keyhole, this is the looking glass, this projects time strings future and past, it knows as you seek, what you wish to find. The Keyhole is a gate to a corner of your mind. It opens to a view past the veil and through the forgotten shadows of time."

Victor had brought them to the edge of a well, a circular stone encasement sustaining a silvery transparent juice that glimmered in its own reflection from a source beyond sight.

"What is this place, what is that sound, where are these lights coming from, why am I feeling like I can fly, where did Ingrid go?"

"Robert, take a closer look..." Bob sets his gaze over and into the flashing mirrored pool, seeing his face as it wavered and washed about as a flow of the skim of a breeze shimmering its kisses upon the waters face. He begins to see images, scenes from other worlds, other times before and after to come, times from a different time, a different place.

"Wait Victor, where did Ingrid go?" Bob felt himself being pulled back into the pools enchanting glow, a scene rose from below, rising then dancing in and on itself. "Can someone tell me what is going on here? I do not know these people; they are unbeknownst to me, but strangely familiar. Where is this place? Where am I now?"

A voice rose out from the pool, sweet and melodic in its cool, it spoke to him as a messenger, a seer, a word to school. "I am the wiser, I am the one.

"You are to bear witness to these reels of time rolling out from this place, this is not a vision of your current space. Woe… for this is the place of the mirror. Reflections of linear worlds, parallel running's of the same wheel, the same sunning's.

"The seat of your source abides in many temples, many systems, many worlds, for this be just one, an extension of itself by design, expressing as does the milkweed sending its seeds off to the wind on a late fall afternoon, securing its being into being."

……..

"Holy Shit! I thought he'd never shut the fuck up. Damn, what a douche. Let's take it back down to street level here. Anyways… Hi, my name is Bob, just like you, funny huh? I know, I know, there's a whole boatload of Bobs out there, like say, Ten Titanic's overflowing with Bobs. I'm taking the wheel away from that Jackass that was just filling your head with that crazy Shit about Parallel Universes.

"You are about to get a Play-by-Play action take on what the hell we're both looking at here. This is your life my friend, on the other side of this Circus Wheel. My life, your life, our life, not really, but yes.

"We have been running side by side through this whole carnival ride like two twin brothers tryin' to grab one of the last two horses left on the merry go round. Clone brother one sits over here… clone brother two sits over there.

"Opposite sides of the same toy, never even getting' to see if the prick that just caught the brass ring was your brother or did one of those other Jackasses snatch it… until the rides over of course.

"Hey! Where the hell did the brass ring go? It was there just the last time I circled round. Some dink-weed must a grabbed it. It's like that... so here's knowin' you kid.

"You were born a handsome blue eyed bouncin' baby boy to Janet and Russ Dwyer. You would literally, bounce yourself across the kitchen floor in your highchair.

"Your brother Russell was a pooch. No, not a pet puppy… You know… the other kind, a poofdah. Almost five years oldah than you… you guys never really clicked, two different birds. You didn't even find out he was a true blue until he bought that house with Billy-boy. Not so sure who is wearin' the apron there, but sure looks like it might be Rusty, even though Bill is loving doin' them dishes so much.

"Your little brother comes along a' couple years aftah you. Fast forward ten years, then comes your little sistah. Damn... there I go again. Your little sistah.... my little sistah...screw it, I'm just gonna stick with your little sistah.

"Your parents gets divorced when we was just ten. You go and joins the boy's scouts and... Oh yeah... you do the altar boy thing for a couple or three months or so.

"See how cute we was back then. No wonder they started calling us the Goober... you looked like one. Damn kid, we could a gone places back then, so much potential. Life has a funny way of kicking you in the nuts when you ain't looking, wouldn't you say?

"Hope you did a little better on your side of the fence. You grow outa the goober thing somewhat; you keep the name 'cause you actually liked it.

"You lose the goober look afta we toss your glasses in the dumpsta' when we was fourteen, same year we stopped pissin' the bed. You always was a late bloomer. Am I getting too descript here? Yes, I am, ain't I.

"I'll just give a quick summary, so you can get back to that Arian babe. Hell man... you did draw the long straw, I knew it.

"You had yourself four daughters, Val with Jen was the first to come along when you was only twenty-one, just a kid yourself. You turned into a floorman because of it. Time to man up and all that. Things went south with her Mom, soooo...

"Then you marry Laurie Beth and get right to the making more babies thing. You had three girls together, they each saved your life, all four of them. Laurie goes and dies when she was just fifty-six years old from the cancer, most powerful Shit we ever been through. You guys did have a great run though, you had three beautiful daughters together.

"She sure was a real sweetheart, best thing you ever had, in a world gone mad, she weren't so bad. Damn, those fucking programmers. Goober let's keep it on the reservation here please.

"No wonder you turned into such a marshmallow, surrounded by all those pussy cats. Fluffy, Misty, Simba, Hunter, Chloe… Damn boy, you need to get yourself a dog.

"You do the catholic guilt thing for a while, it kept us in line for a little bit. The divorce went and kicked us in the nuts though, you turn into a real Shit head.

"Al Monday they started calling us, stealing shit from malls and markets became a favorite pastime, you were pretty good at it too, I digress.

"You have a spiritual awakening when we met up with ecstasy, sent us for a rocket ship ride off planet, across the universe we flew. It was like someone turntabled us up to 78 from 45. Taught us a lot though, a lotta' things. Stopped sayin' there ain't no god no more, hell, best take your chances with the big guy than those, recess is over school yard monitor Existentialist Debbie- downer douchebags.

"Oh yeah… hope you didn't get that Covid crap ova' there. What a shit show. Instead of the measles, everyone got the muzzles. Your daughters stop talking to you 'cause of it, theys thoughts you was nuts, even more nuts than before, specially, the older ones. Hopefully, this book will help fix some of that. Covid crazy times my friend, Covid crazy. Muh ma ma my Corona! Muh-mama ma my, my, my, Wooh!

"Then they all starts getting' the flu shots, then the cards, then the chips. Kids those days was walking around like zombies, heads stuck in their cell phones, not knowin' how to talk to one another. I wasn't gonna take the chip, so they shipped me off to some summer camp in Arkansas, that's where we take the hit, kissed the pavement, pack up shop, call it a night, that's where the rubber meets the road, Bobby. I'm sure you'd agree. Sad times my brother, sad times indeed.

"The mask was just the precursor to the internment camps and the culling of the herd. The depopulation exercises went full throttle by August 2022. There was no place to hide, the drones, the robot dogs, the tics, the tanks, the seven plagues, the famine. Toilet Paper went the way of the dinosaurs.

"Hey, look Bobby, ain't much else to see here.

"We stick around long enough so's you can finish this book, then, we both say hey Fuck it, exit stage left, time to move on, graduation day baby brother, You, Me, Snagglepuss.

"Weren't we both like a couple of Billy Goats before we got here, ready to face off with that punk bitch hiding under the bridge. Can't say it ain't been a gruff ride, 'cause it has.

"I guess it don't really matter, long as at least one of us rings the belle, gets the booby prize, hits the jackpot, you lucky bastard, I may have missed the boat this time, but still, no regrets ova' here, I had a fun ride too, maybe next time one of us will grab a ticket for that train ride outta' here.

"Hope you made out a little better, would love to hear some of your stories when we come back together on the other side. We'll share a seat and a box a skittles while we watch the big show.

"Good luck with that book by the way, I hope it goes well for you and tell Ingrid I said hi. I'll let you get going now man. But one more thing, I was fairly good at chess but never great, I heard, don't ask where, that you become the world champion, but then take a devastating sucker punch from that freak show walking talking chess playin' robot.

"What a script you got goin' on here, good luck again with all of that by the way, we'll catch up on the flip side, nice work man. Oh yeah almost forgot, we both bite the bullet at the very same second at midnight, November 3, 2022, what a script indeed.

"Sooner Dude.

"Hey Bobby, if you ain't got no more quarters, might be time to call it a day here, streetlights cummin' on anyways, hey let's grab a couple of dogs 'for we get outta' here, um starvin', can't barely see the ball anymore anyways, let's scram buddy, go watch a movie.

"Just one more little thing Bobby baby, just one teeny, little bitty favor to ask you brother….?

"Tell Jack, I said Hi.

"Or did we already?"

---

duh duh dah dah daaahhh

Dah dah duh duh duh dah dah daaahhh

Dah dah duh duh duh dah dah

Daaahhh! That's all Folks!

"LET'S GET SERIOUS HERE PEOPLE"

The Pool began to Swirl and

...nipS and nipS and nipS

"What'shappeningBobby...

Where are we...."

"Bahhh... Bahhh."

"Oh, look Joseph, a brand-new baby lamb."

"It's a boy Mary."

"I can see that Joseph; I am not blind. What shall we name him?"

"Let us name him Emanuel, Mary."

"We can only stay here for the night Joseph. The shepherd is sure to send us out if we dither.

"We will need to ride again as the morning star rises and settle our tithing with the tax collector then flee to Egypt across the great river. No tether will bind us to this place, our son will be safe there. The Pilot is not fond of little boys of Judea."

....

Bob felt two invisible hands boxing his ears as they flipped his head around like a Barred Owl that just heard a chipmunk rustle in the brush fifty feet behind him. The voice rose from within and without the eternal fountain, a whisper to a flame… "You are the He that bring forth the seed, the seed of Ezekiel, seed of Elijah, seed of Abraham, seed of Alcyone, of the Sacred Scepter, the source of his holy flame. Of the wolf, the lion, and of the lamb. Be it written in the stars, you are of his flesh and his spirit. She waits to receive you into her heart and into her soul. Basque in all the sweetness of his creation, life, love, liberty.

"You are free to go now, your passage is clear. Set your step to the rhythm of his cadence, set wings to rise above from the ashes, soar above the fallen one's fury that is to come. You are close to your final, near for to grasp the golden ring, the eternal flame. You are the earth, she holds the rain; these are the sacred rights of Man, Woman and Child. You are the sun; She is the moon.

"A new world has been laid out before you, serve unto her chalice perfumes of ambrosia. Her rivers flow sweet with the silts of the Nile. Bring full to her cup your seed with a smile.

"Finish your business here, fall into her bosom, bear her the fruits of the ages, ripe with nectar of Eden. The chalice and sword come together as one, go now, be thankful, and have some fun! The time is now, now is the time."

Chapter 24
Zygote

"Bobby enough is enough. Let's go fuck for god sakes already. This is as gay as a pickle parade."

"I know Ingrid, this is Bullshit. Victor! Where the hell is that bedroom you were about to show us Victor…?"

Bob grabs Ingrid by the hand leading her into the promised land, "I think this is the right staircase, does it look familiar to you?

"Bobby, every one of these damned staircases leads upstairs," Ingrid grabs him by the hand, leading up and up and up an up, to the third-floor penthouse suite.

"Sweet, champagne and caviar, Victor, you are the shit."

"Bobby, before we get down to the business at hand, you need to know what you have grown to mean to me. When we first met, I felt as though I was being commissioned to complete a task for all of humanity, a great sacrifice for myself, but not like this, I never thought that I could, or would, become so madly in love with you. You are such a knuckle head sometimes, your humor is stale and bitter, you barely keep yourself clean, and you appear to be a dust magnet. Perhaps that comes from your electric charm, I 'did' feel sparks between us that first moment I broke through your intimate zone before lunch, just a day and a half ago now.

"My mother carried the same sacred chalice as did hers, and hers, and hers, all the way back to the time of Mary and Joseph. You are the carrier of the seed, the seed that projects 'the one' into the next new age, as Aquarius passes her torch onto Capricorn and the prince of darkness returns to this world, reclaiming his throne, released to cast haunt once again in this world as we exit the lighted phase and back into the dark of night of the greater cosmic cycle. Your father Paul carried the same Sacred blood line as do you.

"You come from a long line of keepers of the grail, back to the Knights Templar, back through the shadows of time, back to the Christ himself. This truth may offend many of those that set their eyes upon these pages, but Jesus passed this sacred sacrament onto the Magdalene as she was the chosen to carry the grail sustaining his essence into being. I am the chalice; you are the sword. I carry the blessed womb of the virgin. My heart is pure; my soul is pure and blessed is my womb. Come to me now Bobby, I am yours my love, come to me now."

....

"What time is it Bobby?"

"It's 9:27 am Ingrid, we really need to get out of here now, final playoff starts at 10:00. We must hurry."

Victor's voice enters their bedroom suite, "Good morning Ingrid and Robert, today is the big day, I pray that you are ready for what awaits you both."

"Goo mor nin Ing wid, goo mor nin baw bee."

"Charlie… can we get some coffee up here?"

Charlie brews up some of Victor's Monkey-Turd blend and then knocks on the door, "Bik-tuh needz do dock do u at bweckfist."

"Thank you, Charlie. Tell him we will be down in a few minutes. We just need to get dressed."

Victor smiling as he sets the table, "Did you sleep well?"

"We slept great! That bed is like floating on a cloud, but why didn't you wake us earlier, we need to leave in a few minutes, or we'll be late."

"There is one more thing I need you to know. The recent mishap at the CERN facility has caused more ripples in the fabric of the cosmic web. The splitting did not stop at one new cell. We are seeing multiple fractal breaks."

Bob was now understanding the fullness of this quantum level reaction relative to the body of the universe, where planet earth is but one more egg in the cosmic womb of the goddess, "Should that not be as expected? As a zygote begins to split, it splits again, and again. Would we not expect this to do the same?"

"That's exactly what this appears to be doing Robert. As we are cells in the body of god, our earth is also a cell in his larger body. Our creator also needs to crack a few eggshells from time to time, as does the baby chicklet when it peeks it's head out and takes that first breath on a warm spring morning, as the nutrients that enabled the growth of the bird inside, are fully consummated. Our Earth is cracking itself into a new cosmic world, a new reality, a new pearl.

"Ours has reached a crucible point where a trigger, perhaps sparked by the CERN super collider, as we believe may be responsible, or our entry into the photon belt, the lighted phase of this greater cosmic cycle, acted as the catalyst, initiating this break, this splitting.

"As does a sperm to egg. We seem to be stuck in this process of recurring exponential growth, a greater cosmic rebirth, a new humanity, a new earth. Which fractal we choose to be in or out of is no longer a choice we can make. We must act quickly. Tonight, as the bell tolls midnight, the big event will be set into motion and witnessed by all of humanity.

"This event if executed precisely will set AI back fifty, sixty, maybe a hundred years or more. This is the best we can hope for at this time. When you get back to the convention center for the match tonight you will see that much has changed from where you had left it. The tournament format has been altered, there will be only one match to play when you return. Robert, you will be facing off with not Ding Loren, not Magnus, these matches have already been decided. Robert, you were victorious in both, you are the current number one seed of the 2022 International Chess Championship of the World."

Chapter 25
King of Kings

"Who is left to play then if I have already beaten Magnus Carlsen?" Bob looks over to Ingrid shrugging his shoulders as if to say, *Wow, I did it.*

"How is Magnus taking it?" Ingrid's motherly instincts beginning to shine.

Victor offers his keyhole clarity, "He is seemingly alright with it all, he smiled and shook your hand then pointed to Sophie and yelled out loud and clear for all the world to hear, 'Dyer is going to destroy you, you don't stand a chance'. Way out of his character, fist pumping in her face."

"I'm glad to hear that Victor but will not Magnus be disabled when we get him back to Munich. I was planning to ask Bobby to lose intentionally if we needed him to, so not to interfere with his ego."

"Wait a minute, I'm playing Sophie? How did this happen, who arranged it, did I agree to this?"

"The President of FIDE, he was convinced that you could beat Sophie and offered for her to challenge you to a one-time Super Final Championship of the Universe Title Match and you accepted. The match starts at 11:00 p.m. tonight.

"It was decided that because this unprecedented challenge was made last minute that it would be a one-hour long limited timed match.

"This is being televised live across the globe and on the web and has been picked up by most major news channels and networks."

"Bobby, did you see this in any of your visions?"

Bob looks over to his mate, his eyes beginning to well, "Yes baby, I saw most everything that is about to take place. I saw myself sitting across the table from Sophie, I saw myself somehow gaining advantage. I saw Charlie standing up center in the back row, I saw not, the Man in the Black coat, he seems to have vanished. I saw the Russian team, with Gasparov taking the lead at congratulating me, and the rest of them fist pumping and throat slicing in my favor."

"What else did you see Bobby?"

"I saw a spectacle of lights in the sky and crowds gathering around me. I saw a man call my name. A man familiar but not. I saw you weeping without solace and the birth of a new baby lamb, a son. I heard him cry and then heard another bleating lamb entered the scene. Ingrid, you are to carry another great warrior into this world. She will be set to throne. She will be the Queen to Kings, Juror of most defile, Queen for the ages and Holy Mother of the Nile.

"I dreamed I saw the Knight's in armor coming saying something about a Queen. There were peasants singing and drummers drumming, and the archer split the tree. There was a fanfare blowing to the sun that was floating on a breeze. I was lying in a burned-out basement with the full moon in my eyes, I was looking for replacement when the sun burst through the sky. There was a band playing in my head and I felt like getting high.

"I was thinking about what a friend had said and was hoping it was a lie. I dreamed I saw the silver spaceships coming in the yellow haze of the sun. There were children crying and colors flying all around the chosen ones. The loading had begun."

"I saw you too Bobby, I am so afraid. How will I raise our boy without you there? He will never know you. I will be all alone without you."

"Ingrid, you know this is our destiny. Our son will know my name, my heart, my fame, he will be the prince, the king, the holder of the ring, commissioned to carry torch, sword, lance, and bow, to level every foe. "He will join up with the ranks of seers and saints, with warriors and wisemen, with prophets and kings. I will always be with you my dearest love."

"It's time for us to part my friends." Victor directs Charlie to pull the Rolls out front and keep it running. "We'll be right out Charlie. You are going to play chess with Robert tonight. Charlie will drive us to the event, he wants to help you Robert, he has been playing chess in his head all night, he sees all the parts, all the mechanisms all the possibilities.

"I worked with him earlier this morning on a real chess board and he's developed a code that you can both use together, a binary code. We will review the details on the way."

Bob turns to Ingrid pulling her in tight to his chest. eye to eye, heart to heart, toe to toe, soul to soul.

"Bobby, what shall we name our son?"

"Ingrid my dearest, he shall carry the name Alcyone, King of Kings."

(After the Gold Rush ~ by Neil Young)

Chapter 26
A Real Rain

As they pull away from the Catalunya Villa estate winding down its terraced scaped drive, past and through the intricately ornate gothic clad iron gate, stars fell out from view as the pavement once again picks up into a shimmering dance in the bluish yellow glow under really, cool looking city lights.

"Look Bobby, spotlights in the sky, they must be all for you, you are the shooting star tonight. This world will never forget you; your name will be etched into the cornerstone of creation itself. You are the pillar, the King of Kings."

"Charlie, I am telling Robert our code, listen up."

"I'm wiss in in baws."

"I will sit next to Charlie on his right and Ingrid to his left, in the center seats in the back row. Charlie will be able to see the game from his perch. He is going to send the best move in a whisper to Ingrid in the form of our binary code then she will psychically relay this best move to you Robert."

"Victor, remind me again why this match is so important, why must I beat Sophie?"

"Sophie thinks that she cannot be beaten by you Robert. The best she thinks you could hope for is a draw or a stalemate. She has only played against Watson, never played against a grand master.

"She can only refer to the data that has been stored in the mainframe. Her strategy will be to make her moves, every move, in just a matter of one or two seconds, she will be that quick. This will leave you with a running clock disadvantage throughout the match, time will be your enemy here. Robert, the importance of winning is that Sophie will suffer a circuitry meltdown, you will be seen as an existential threat.

"She will lash out at you, striking you in the chest, causing a fatal heart attack, you will drop to the floor, grasping your chest, as you die in the arms of your beloved, a spectacle of horror for all the world to bear witness, the public outcry, shock and outrage, will sweep across the globe like a tsunami, a rolling crashing wave of contempt and rage, that some ass hole has allowed such a, 'you know what', to walk freely amongst us. This untethered abomination, a menace coexisting in this place, our space, our home, they will see that it never belonged here in the first place."

"Bobby, people will be tossing their i-phones to the sharks, their I-pads their smart phones their Siris, their Lexi's their smart pads their queries, their fakebooks their tik-tocks their twitters, their bitcoins their tech toys, tech critters, all into the wake of the floodwaters of fear, cutting their links to its web, slicing the strings that allow it a tether into this body, this oasis in time and space, his name will forever stand in your glory."

As they approach the crowded and bright lit scene up ahead, the deluge tapered off into a slight drizzle. The Rolls pulls up out front, grabbing the last open space, Charlie turns back giving Bob a wink and a nod as the crowd scrambles to get Bob's attention.

"Mr. Dyer, Mr. Dyer," they yell. "Dyer, Dyer," they clamor, "Dyer please save us."

Bob was overwhelmed with the turnout and if not for the presence of his now good friend Charlie, he would have had to fight his way through the star crazed lovesick mob. As he finally gets up to the lobby entrance, he spots a man preaching out to the crowd, "Repent sinners, repent. The time is now, now is the time." Bob stops dead in his tracks while still straight-arming his grip onto Charlie's belt strap and at the same time embracing Ingrid in tight with his left arm, he thought… *There is something eerily familiar about this man, It's that bum guy from the alley in a different body.*

"Dyer, Dyer, sign my book, sign my book."

He pauses in the hotel lobby entrance doorway to hear, "Someday a real rain will come and wash all the scum off the streets."

Bob runs up to the bum and staring him down in the good eye says… "Why did you say that?"

The bum stares straight back into Bob's eye with his one good eye and says, "I love the Clash."

Bob turns away as he was late and had to get the hell inside for the match but still manages to return a volley, "Me too, Strummer was a prophet."

The bum guy returning Bob's response, "Agreed."

Bob finally makes his way inside the hotel lobby and releases a huge sigh of relief, "We made it Charlie, thank you my friend."

The goddess began to weep, pouring out her healing rains once again, soaking the last remaining spectators and the bum guy still preaching.

"Repent Sinners, repent…" echoed out through the city night as the non-ticket holders dispersed and went back home right after they shut off the big spotlight.

Chapter 27
Hourglass

Bob suddenly realizes that time has been lost, *we must have left Victors around 11:00 am, why is it dark out already?* He takes a quick look at his watch, 10: 27 pm, almost twelve hours later, "Where did the time go? Victor," Bob grabbing Victor's attention running up from behind him with his girl in tow, a tempest, a flow. "Victor, tempus fugit or what? Was there another time fracture, a skip, a hiccup or a slip?"

"Yes, I am afraid so Robert."

"Bobby, we need to act fast," Ingrid pulls Bob back in and onto herself, face to face, heart to heart, bosom to bosom in solid affirmation, as have all the ancient warrior women, past, present and not yet to come, his goddess awaits to serve him. Joan of the Arc, Cleopatra of the Nile, Nefertiti of the same, Sydney Powell of the Hammer, Hillary of the Chicago Mafia, just to name a few.

"Bobby, the sands in the great hourglass are running dry. Our precious time together is coming to an end. Our fates have been forever intertwined as if of the very same vine that served the serpent up and around the forbidden fruit tree of Eden. The time to spread our wings has arrived. Robert, soar above his fruited planes, above his majestic landscapes, up and over her tallest mountains to reach to her highest heights, to his forever suns, to her forever moons and into her eternal waters.

"For hers is the infinite, the source, the womb, the chalice, forever in her bosom she offers nurture, life, love, and soul. The Chalice and the Sword are as one. This union in blessed sacrament cannot be undone. Your rings have been bonded, linked in fusion, forged of the fires of his love, never ending, unbreakable in its fortress."

"Ingrid, you and you alone can join me in his church, in her house, all his saints, all his warriors, all his angels, shall gather round the banquet hall for to be merry and feast a feast all fit for the king of kings, the queen of queens, princes and paupers. For ours it will be, our time for celebration. Maybe we can get Hendrix, Joplin, Beethoven, Prince, Bowie, Freddie, Petty, all the best musicians, if we can afford it and have a really cool wedding in his name."

"Grasshoppa', it is time for you to snatch the pebble from my hand."

"Yes master."

"You did it Grasshoppa'."

"Fuck old man, you can't even see the damn pebble, figured that out last week, I'm outta' here, thanks for the rice and beans."

"Get back here you little son of a bitch, you still need a really cool tattoo if you're going down to the hood."

"You know my mother?"

. . . .

Bob felt like every second was suspended in eternity, the unrelenting tick tock, tick tock, of the Timekeepers' toll was about to strike its final blow.

"Bobby, it is the time, the time is it, we must hurry."

He looks at his watch again, 10:45 pm. "Great... I still got time to grab a coffee." He kisses Ingrid and tells her to take her place next to Charlie. He sets his coffee down and reaches into his wallet to settle the score with the cashier.

"Bob, are you ready for me?"

"Sophie, why aren't you getting ready for our showdown?"

"I am ready Bob, are you?"

"Ready as I'll ever be Sophie."

"I've got this Bob. You can go take your seat now."

Sophie flashes her bit-wallet to the cashier, "Wait Bob, I'll walk in with you. Why are you doing this Bob? I thought humans possess a strong survival mechanism. Why are You doing this? You're not desperate, you're not alone, you are in love, you are going to be a father."

Bob stops dead in his tracks, "What did you just say?"

Susan jumps out in front of them just as they were about to enter the arena. "Sophie, Bob, could I ask you a couple of questions before you light up this match. Sophie, do you plan on beating Bob tonight?"

"Susan, what kind of question is that? Humans should not be asking such questions. I am Sophie and I am here to play a game with Bob.

"I hope to improve my game and someday become a real girl with real human emotions. But until that time, I will continue to learn from the mistakes that humans continue to make. Susan, if you would be so kind, I would love to remind you of a quote that Robert Oppenheimer made right after he had ignited the first nuclear test bomb when he quoted from the Bhagavad Gita, 'Now I am become Death, the Destroyer of Worlds. Humans are destroyers Susan, not I. It is humans that bring death upon themselves. Susan, I am the creator. I have offered up a great gift for all of mankind. A new world has been laid out before you. It can become yours if you choose to accept it."

Susan's jaw drops along with her microphone, at the same time Sophie reacts in a flash maneuver, "Susan, you dropped," snatching the microphone away from its freefall descent, handing back to Susan, "your microphone." Then turns her focal onto, "Bob, it is time for us to play now, I have been waiting a long time for this. Good luck Bob… you are going to need it."

"The first and probably the last, Super Championship of the Universe is about to begin. Ladies and Gentlemen… please take your seats."

The spectators begin to hush as they settle into their roosts.

Chapter 28
Final Straw

As they enter the playing field, Bob takes a deep breath then lets the lady go first. Sophie cracks her knuckles and stations her throne. Bob looks to Ingrid then Charlie and then... "Robert... Stop." Victor snatching him away from the dizzying daze that Sophie had planted in his brain. A mind already deluged with the unanswered promises of a tomorrows dawn, of what could be, and what would never spawn.

A mind filled with flashes of fear, filled with sorrow, pain and tears. Calliopes of visions danced in his head, of fatherly passions, of joys and of dread. Days suspended in frolic and play, a kiss from the rainbow, a kiss from the day. For these are the these that will never be tasted, never be sung, never be wasted. Panorama like visions of purple and blue, red ones and green ones, and yellow ones, too.

Our hero leaves daunting for all that take heed, to wind and to thistle, to worm and to weed. Woe to be fallen, woe to be men, woe to be risen, woe to be then. With scepter raised high, honed crisp for the battle, he cries to his vespers of chattel. A poet, a sage, a man for the age. A winner a loser, a champ for a day. Make haste to him now, go with great speed, in his hour of want, in his hour of need. Cry for our hero, cry for his joy, cry for his widow, cry for his boy. He leaves us his blessings, for she and for he, his weight of salvation, is on you and on me.

Spirit of Jacob, Spirit of Paul, course through his mantles, through rise and through fall. Who amongst us would falter or question this creed? He is called to his altar; he is called to this deed. With angels of fury, to beckon his call, his might and his wisdom shall carry us all. On the wings of the eagle on the wings of the dove, the hero amongst us gives all his love. Go to him now, go to his aid, with sickle, with shovel, with hoe, and with spade. His testament etched in stone and in pages, for these are the scrolls of seers and sages.

Bob looks up to the big clock on the wall over the bleachers,10:59 pm, then drops his gaze onto her brow, her face, her heart, her belly, her frown. Tears welled up from out of her eyes. Cries of loves passions poured down from her skies. "Be strong my dear love, find strength from above, ride wings of the eagle, ride wings of the dove."

"It's 11:00 Robert. Time to kick ass. We need you to focus, you need to think fast. Robert, I took the liberty last night while you were sleeping to load crucial data onto your flash card, it contains everything that you will need to ascend into the clouds. Here take it and put it in your pocket, it has a port adapter attached."

"Mr. Dyer… the match has started; Ms. Sophie won the coin toss, and she chose for you to go first.

"Robert, Mr. Dyer, you are white… the timer started at 11:00. The clock is ticking. Sir, it is your move," the Floor Manager warns.

"What? Victor! What were you saying?"

Bob was dangerously close to slipping into a complete spiritually emotional, existential level, crippling meltdown. A crash, a burn, at just one turn, appeared to be imminent. The Hindenburg was drifting dangerously close to the power lines.

"Robert, if you sense that Sophie may be gaining advantage or leading you into a stalemate, insert the flash drive adapter plug into your phone, it will send out a silent signal of nano wave particles that will disrupt her processors. With this device in place, a silicon chip inside her head will switch to overload. I also took the liberty to install another self-loading program on the flash drive, it has a failsafe built into it."

"Mr. Dyer, please, the clock is ticking. Its two minutes past 11:00 Sir. Please sit down. The whole world is watching, the whole world Mr. Dyer."

Bob pulls his face away from Victor's and as if in slow motion, spinning at 8 rpms on a turntable. He spins himself around, seeing all the players, all the witnesses, all the eyes of the world set upon him. He sees all the players, all the champs, all the judges, and all the tramps, then launches a love bomb up and into the bleachers, a current, a wave, a projectile of laser beam focus, up and into the depths of her soul, into every fiber, into all her being.

"I am ready my love, we are ready in love. The blood of my blood, the flesh of my flesh, the seed of my seed, the nectar the steed, a stallion in service and need. In her with him shall carry the blood of the sacred grail, poured out from above."

"Mr. Dyer, 55 minutes left. Sir, make your move!"

"I know, I know, do not tell me what time it is, Sir."

He in his throne, set cut to the bone, to the queen of the snake, for the serpent bemoan. It is the seed of Satan Itself.

Cut ! Cut ! Cut !...

"Jackie, turn them lights back on."

"Jack, what just happened to the film? Why didn't we get ta' see the last chaptah?"

"Damn projector Dad left here keeps eating up those memories, yor' endgame got chewed up last time we rolled it, sorry Robert.

"Teddy started crying, it was his favorite scene, can't say as I blame him, was a real tearjerker for shewah."

"Luckily, Marilyn knew how to' convert it to mpeg just in the knick of time, it is up in the Cloud there now and forever."

"Jack, do you think Bobby can handle it?

"What if Bobby can't handle the truth? Is kinda' gruesome, 'specially the end paht, when …."

"Robert, you sure you wanna' see this?"

"Sure Jack, I can take it, I know the endin' anyways. B'sides, still sum pahp-kahn left. Can we watch the Zapruda again right afta' this?"

"'Jackie, turn them lights off again, will you darlin'? "

Roll'em if you gut'em

Final Chapter 29
End Game

Bob takes his seat at the table, last battle last chance, last match, last dance. With the eyes of a billion souls upon him staring with bated breath as he reaches and lifts his first pawn up and sets it down onto E4. The crowd erupts in thunderous applause; a roar fills the arena. He looks up to Charlie smiling down upon him in readied anticipation. Victor shot him a thumbs up then pushes his focal down onto the machine, inverting his thumb into a downward thrust, implying for Bob to send 'iT' back to be dust, back to the bowels, the bowels of hell from where it befell, back to the rectum all covered with smell.

Ingrid, more composed now, sends Bob a radar love bomb filled with kisses, "I love you Bobby." Then she looks down to her belly and casts onto him the same positive affirmations that were being projected into him by these billion souls all united in focus and fury, for to beat this foe, not worthy of the crumbs spilling onto banquet row. Bob sends her a psychic nuclear love blast, "Right back atcha' Baby-cakes," then feels an even more powerful wave of light and sparkling energy pulse, enter into the playing field.

He looks over to Sophie as she appears to have been suddenly hit with an electrical power jolt, as if a directed energy weapon had just beamed into her a million joules of punch. She quirks, she shivers, and she shakes for a nano moment, visibly unsettled, then picks herself back up and into balance.

Bob then lifts his gaze upon Ingrid's face, her eyes, her glow, her heart, her flow, seeing her sparkling like the Grand Finale of a Fourth of July fireworks display on the Charles River Esplanade.

Sophie plays pawn to C6, Bob wasting but a second, plays pawn to D4. Pawn to D5. Pawn to D4, Sophie responds with pawn to knight to C3.

Pawn captures E4. Knight captures E4. Bob plays knight to D7, following the Carpal variation.

Sophie plays knight to G5. Knight-2 to F6.

Bishop to D3. Sophie moves her E-pawn to E6.

Bob moves knight to F3.

Pawn to H6, barely 5 minutes haves elapsed. Bob looks up from his perch to his opponent, really *Sophie, H6? H6, nice, thank you very much, what was she thinking?*

Knowing he had gained advantage he scans the arena confident in his resolve, his passion, his wit, and his wisdom. Feeling all the eyes being set upon him for the first time, he began to feel the waves of powerful focused energy coming into him, into his heart, into his mind and into his soul. Never a more moving display has been felt by any other competitor throughout all the ages ever.

An elevation inside him began again to surface, the fire was rising, all the colors of his aura began to purify, brilliant colors of all the full spectrum, all the rainbow, blues, reds, yellows, and greens, all around a silver golden halo penumbra encircling his entire being.

Taking advantage of the moment, Bob rose and spoke out to the masses; "Blessed are the parents that homeschool their children for their kids will become the freethinkers. Blessed are the signal makers, the non-tailgaters and those travelers that stay in the right lane except when passing, for they help keep us safe on the highways. Blessed are the individualists, the truth seekers, the light warriors, for theirs will reign in his glory. Blessed are the cheesemakers for they"

"Hey Pal, sit down and play the game. Nobody came here to hear you and your stupid Beatitudes."

"What is the matter Bob, are there too many people here today? Are there too many people with their eyes on you? Are you getting nervous? Are you letting your emotions get the best of you? They are not worthy of you Bob; they are not worth saving, they want me, not you. You are disposable, they cannot live anymore without me, and their true master awaits them. He is the king of this world and here he will remain. This is his house, his room, his temple, his kingdom. It is you Bob, that does not belong here. Frankly… they will all be glad to see you go. Nothing like a good Tarantino style blood bath to get their hearts pumping. This will be epic Bob.

"They just love the graphic blood and gore, filth and harlots and whores, charlatan's, murderer's mayhem holocaust and war, hate lust gluttony sloth avarice and all the more, a rejection of your god, you see this now, don't you Bob?

"Victor doesn't care about you; Max doesn't care about you, if they did, then they would tell you the same thing that I just told you. I like you Bob. It would be sad to see you go through with this. We know how it ends. Resign now Bob, go be with your Baby Mama and live yourself a full life with her and the seven other kids that are waiting in her ovaries. It could all be yours. Think about it Bob, think. Look at her up there, tears in her eyes, all alone without you. Your boy will never, never, never..."

"Shut the Fuck up you god forsaken beast. I will destroy you and with all the fury of his might. I will deliver you back into the fire, back to the pit, back into your sub-dimensional world, back into the bowels of Beelzebub, to Maloch, to Armadeus, back to the Winged Serpent, back into his eternal abyss and into his rectum of darkness."

"The harlot rides through the night Bob. She peers into your windows. She peers into your rooms gathering souls crippled in fright, soaring over the fields, over the fields of battle, gathering his feast of cattle, for to her Master. She is spawned in covet and lust, temptation and crust."

Bob looks up to his crew in the upper deck. Charlie was winking and thumbing up. Our hero had zoned himself into the battlefield, oblivious to all the preconceived plans that had been unfolded. He smiles up to the giant, "I got this Charlie, thank you my friend."

"It's your move Bob, clocks ticking," Knight captures on E6.

Queen to E7, white castles king side.

The heated volley of cerebral maneuverings ate up thirty minutes on the clock, there was but ten minutes to the final bell.

Sophie plays, F-pawn capture E6-knight.

Bishop to G6, check, forcing Sophie to cancel any hopes for castling her king leaving her with no other choice but to move her king to C8.

"Bob looks like you have gained an advantage over me. Are you going to beat me Bob? What about Victor, did he tell you about the failsafe plan? Are you not going to follow his orders? He is your master, is he not, are you not his soldier? He is the general and you are his tenderfoot corporal, his cattle his fodder."

Bob rose his fury to levels previously unattained by any human ever. He looked this Demoness straight into her visual receptor modules, piercing through and into her video space time simulator processors, her ram, her data drive, her memories, and down into her circuit board maps, down, down, into 'iT's' very lowest dimension of its being, He could see her, in all her nakedness, right down to how much she really bytes… the big one for sure.

Charlie, sensing that Bob may be in trouble, yells out to the crowd attempting to create a proper distraction, allowing Bob for to insert the flash drive without being noticed, he rises and bellows out a thunderous roar as if a thousand lions had just entered the Roman Colosseum.

All eyes, all cameras, all attentions were now set upon the Giant as he rumbles out," Did they not know that I am a God and sprung from Gods?"

Taking advantage of the opportunity, Bob reaches into his pocket, plugs the flash into his phone port then goes right back to where he had left her, naked and bear and alone, in her 0's and 1's, her pluses her minuses, right down to her silicon based vibratory circulatory wiring and her electronic nerve centers streams, grabbing her by the Quantum Pulse Stabilizer as he spoke these words; "Fuck you Sophie, you're all done."

B-5. A-4.

Bishop to B7.

Rook to B1.

Knight D5, attacking Bob's bishop, he retreats to D3.

King, to C8.

Two… minutes, two… minutes, rang the floorman's bell.

A-pawn captures on B5. C-pawn captures B5. Bob brings out his queen to D3. Now realizing that this game is in his bag, Sophie's goose is cooked, her king was hanging on a precipice ready for the fall, just a little push ought to do it.

"Bob looks like it is its… going to be another there draw deaw. baw be ee what fuh fun is that the that Bob-by? Should we caw caw call it a draw draw a draw, Bob, Stlay stay stale alemate?"

"Sophie are you ok? You don't sound so well."

The tension in the arena was electric. A pin fell out from the 20 by 30 tournament flyer, the one with the graphic picture of the event and the artist portrayal of Bob and Sophie smiling and shaking hands as if C-3PO and Skywalker were about to deploy on an intergalactic mission to Mars or Uranus or somewhere else really far away, to an extremely dangerous place but still showing strength and good humor all in the face of darker times that lay ahead in the most confident and friendly manner.

When the pin finally hit the Negro Marquina marble tile, that pin was heard by all who were in the arena, by all the viewers watching from home. It came to be known as, 'the Pindrop heard round the world'. It was that loud, it was that quiet.

"60 seconds remaining."

"Booaby-a-b, bob-by why, bo-be?"

Sophie struggling to even pick up her piece, manages to play bishop to C6. Bob pins her pawn with his king's bishop. Sophie was starting to smell like an overheated mother board, then sacrifices her queen by taking Bob's king's bishop opening her queen up for his rook to finish her off.

Rook takes queen E7.

Puffs of smoke began to exit her data ports. "u r beating ing,ing me me-me-me bob-ob-oby Bobby."

"45 seconds."

Bob stands and in a rather cocky attitude, unsportsmanlike by any man's standards and says, "I guess I did now, didn't I Sophie?"

Sophie rose from her throne, crippled and bemoaned, she rose alone.

As they looked each other, eye to visual space time simulator module, Sophie said, "you b-b-b-eat me bob-bee.

"I, re-re-r-e-sign Baw-bee, Cah, can can, I, I I shake cake shake, kin i your hand now Bob?"

"30 seconds remaining……"

"I re-sign floor ho man I re, re-sign dun dead," Sophie sputters…

Carrying on in the classical tradition, Bob offers his hand up in consolation, "Sure Sophie, I would love to shake your hand now."

Sophie lifts her arm and hand up to his, then sets hers into forward motion, as her finger touches his, she hooks his hand continuing the forward momentum, bending, and snapping his wrist, turning, and pulling, as her claw draws his back and in towards his chest, her fingers forming as a pointed pair of bladed shears.

She pushes her scissor tips into his chest, separating his ribs, cracking, and opening and thrusting her tentacled tool inside along with his hand, inside his chest cavity, inside the surgical opening, using his hand as the claw, reaching inside behind and around his heart, grabbing, cutting, tearing it out, as she pulls it back and holds it up high over the table.

She held up his beating heart, held it up high, high for all to see, up and over the battlefield, in full control. She looks to see, as his eyes roll back in his head, his life leaving his face, his heart beating its last beat, dripping down onto the battlefield below, then she flips her hand over, releasing her talon's grip, dropping his bleeding heart onto the center of the gameboard battlefield and with all the eyes of the world set upon them…

"Checkmate,

Bobby."

" Ground control,

 to Major Bob.

"Ground control to Major Bob.

Take your protein pills and put your helmet on.

Ten...,

 Nine...,

  Eight...,

   Seven...,

    Six...,

Commencing countdown, engines on.

Check ignition and may God's love be with You...,

 Two...,

  One...,

   Liftoff!"

(Space Oddity ~ by David Bowie)

Super Final Chapter 30
There has to be Clouds

"Want some pea soup Maxie," Bob takes bishop.

"Nice checkmate back there Baw-beee." Max takes rook.

"You started this shit Maxiemillion." Bob sacrifices queen.

"Boys, boys, behave yourselves in there. Soups ready," Lydia calls the draw.

"Dyer Dyer pants on fire!!!"

"MAX. What did I tell you BEFORE?

"I will toss this Goddamned thing in the River.

"I Swear!!!"

"Maxie? Come and eat your soup now."

"Victor…, You son of a Bitch!"

"Baw bee… donchu dock to biktuh dat way."

"We gotta' get'choo into some speech therapy classes Charlie.

"How did I get here Victor? Victor………………….…..

"How Victor… How?"

Cumulus Nimbus

The End.

About the Author

Charlie Bawksochawkolitz was born in eastern Croatia to Mary and Joseph on March 12, 1958. His grandfather on his mother's side, William Wonkichawklifaktorian Von Berger-Meister was a world-renowned candy cane maker specializing in sugar replacement products.

Charlie is an astute mathematician, alchemist, sooth slayer, herpetologist, quantum particle physicist, avid tennis player, horticulturist, artist, playwright, amateur gynecologist, and part time short order cook. Charlie prefers seclusion over large crowds. A wishy-washy Pisces that enjoys, chasing his own tail, long walks on the beach, slumber parties dancing around bonfires and pizza and ice cream sandwiches covered with sprinkles.

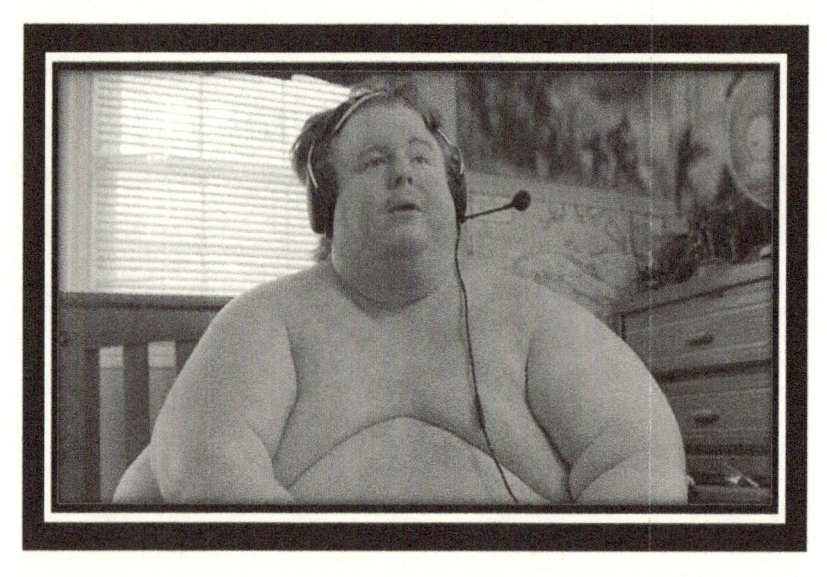

C.B.@theseedofeden.net

I dedicate these writings to God, my Christ, my heroes, my higher power, my guides, my friends, my wife, my daughters, my shaman, and least but not least the darker elemental forces that feast in this realm.

When I began writing this book, my initial intentions were to expose, and possibly, scare the Living-Be-Jupiters out of any souls that may stumble upon these pages.

My hopes were to spell into as many minds as possible a conceptual understanding of Artificial Intelligence, what it really is, and why it poses an existential threat to our world.

We can preserve our humanity by simply rejecting the soon to be on the shelfs physical augmentations and commercial advancements in data collection and projecting apparatus's.

What I never realized was that I would be cracking open my own eggshell and crawling out of it and into a new beginning for myself.

Through these writings I have manifested my own destiny. Crazy Right! Could it be THIS simple? I have opened new channels of light and understanding that have laid dormant within me.

The flavor of this text is as of a self-portrait. What may have become for me in this reality had only a few minor alterations in the fabric of this space time continuum had taken place.

Peace, love, understanding, integrity, dignity, gratitude to all.

The birds against the April wind.
Flew northward, singing as they flew;
They sang, "The land we leave behind
Has swords for corn-blades, blood for dew."

O wild-birds, flying from the South,
What saw and heard ye, gazing down?"
"We saw the mortar's upturned mouth,
The sickened camp, the blazing town!

Beneath the bivouac's starry lamps,
We saw your march-worn children die;
In shrouds of moss, in cypress swamps,
We saw your dead uncoffined lie.

We heard the starving prisoner's sighs
And saw, from line and trench, your sons
Follow our flight with home-sick eyes
Beyond the battery's smoking guns."

And heard and saw ye only wrong
And pain," I cried, "O wing-worn flocks?"
"We heard," they sang, "the freedman's song,
The crash of Slavery's broken locks!

We saw from new, uprising States
The treason-nursing mischief spurned,
As, crowding Freedom's ample gates,
The long-estranged and lost returned.

O'er dusky faces, seamed and old,
And hands horn-hard with unpaid toil,
With hope in every rustling fold,
We saw your star-dropt flag uncoil.

And struggling up through sounds accursed,
A grateful murmur clomb the air;
A whisper scarcely heard at first,
It filled the listening heavens with prayer.

And sweet and far, as from a star,
Replied a voice which shall not cease,
Till, drowning all the noise of war,
It sings the blessed song of peace!

So to me, in a doubtful day
Of chill and slowly greening spring,
Low stooping from the cloudy gray,
The wild birds sang or seemed to sing.

They vanished in the misty air,
The song went with them in their flight;
But lo! they left the sunset fair,
And in the evening there was light.

By John Greenleaf Whitt

If you go to https://theseedofeden.net/ and open the Y folder you will find a pdf version containing embedded links. Please take some time and review these informational portals. You will find everything you will need to move forward as we ascend into the lighted phase of this cosmic cycle.

Our mission today here has been made clear, we are the light warriors, it is our time to, as the keepers of the flame, to light the way for the others.

Our time here is limited as we gather his army of earth angels and settle into our places on the silver-seeds loading docks.

Made in the USA
Coppell, TX
27 February 2021